Into the Death Tube

Han Solo drove his swoop into the weather station's giant emission cylinder. The pursuing craft hung back a moment, then followed.

"Stay gripped!" he called to the woman behind him, jockeying the swoop to face his enemies. They scattered, then dropped onto his tail again, ready to trap him at the cylinder's far end.

Han speeded up once more. The engine pod blared its power. The end of the emission cylinder was swinging, first revealing and then concealing meter-and-a-half-wide openings in the gridwork as it moved. The opening Han had selected expanded before him as he drove toward it. There was a terrible moment of doubt . . . then the gridwork passed him like a shadow, and they were in the open.

He took a quick look behind. Pieces of wreckage were raining slowly toward the ground; one of his pursuers had tried to emulate him and failed . . .

Also by Brian Daley
Published by Ballantine Books:

HAN SOLO AT STARS' END
THE DOOMFARERS OF CORAMONDE
THE STARFOLLOWERS OF CORAMONDE

HAN SOLO'S REVENGE

From the Adventures of
Luke Skywalker

by Brian Daley

Based on the characters and
situations created by

George Lucas

A Del Rey Book

BALLANTINE BOOKS • NEW YORK

For Cargo-master-apprentice Dane Thorson,
Chief Scout Adam Reith, Jason dinAlt, Jame
Retief of the *Corps Diplomatique Terrestrienne*
and all others of that rare stripe

And who are they anyway, these so-called free traders and independent spacers? Rogues, scoundrels, and worse! The common slangtalk term "freighter bums" is more applicable, surely. Beware to the shipper who would entrust them with cargo; woe to the being who books passage with them!

At best, they are feckless ruffians whose unconscionable social values allow them to undercut the fee rates of established, reliable companies. More often, they're con artists, frauds, tariff-dodgers and, yes, even smugglers!

Is any rascal with a spacecraft to be entrusted with your livelihood? Overhead, administrative apparatus, and managerial proprieties—these are the best guaranties of a dependable business arrangement!

(Excerpted from Public Service Message #122267-50, sponsored by the Corporate Sector Authority)

I

"CHEWIE, hey, I've got it!"

Han Solo's happy shout surprised Chewbacca so much that the towering Wookiee straightened involuntarily. Since he'd been hunkered down under the belly of the starship *Millennium Falcon* welding her hull with a plasma torch, he bumped his shaggy head against her with a resounding gong.

Snapping off the torch and letting its superheated field die, the Wookiee tore off his welding mask and threw it at his friend. Han, knowing Chewbacca's temper, skidded to a stop and ducked with the reflexes of a seasoned star pilot as the heavy mask zipped by overhead. He took a step backward as Chewbacca stalked out from under the grounded *Falcon* into the brilliant light of Kamar's white sun. Making temporary repairs on the damaged ship had brought the Wookiee peevishly close to mayhem.

Han pulled off his wraparound sun visor and grinned, raising his free hand to ward off his copilot's pique.

"Hold on, hold it. We've got a new holofeature; Sonniod just brought it." To prove it, Han held up the cube of clear material. Chewbacca forgot his anger for the moment and made a lowing, interrogative sound.

"It's some kind of musical story or something," Han replied. "The customers probably won't understand this one either, but are we going to pack them in now! Music, singing, dancing!"

Han, waving the cube, beamed happily over their good fortune. He still retained a good deal of the ranginess of youth, but combined it with much of the confidence of maturity. He had shucked his vest in the heat of Kamar, and his sweat-stained pullover shirt clung to his chest and back. He wore high space-man's boots and military-cut trousers with red piping on their seams. At his side was a constant companion, a custom-made blaster that was fitted with a rear-mounted macroscope. Its front sight blade had been filed off with the speeddraw in mind. Han wore it low and tied down at his right thigh in a holster that had been cut away to expose his sidearm's trigger and trig-ger guard.

"Chewie, we're gonna be pulling in customers from all over the Badlands!"

With a noncommittal grunt Chewbacca went to pick up the fallen plasma torch. Kamar's sun was lowering at the horizon, and he'd done just about all he could to make the ship spaceworthy anyway.

He was large, even for a Wookiee—an immense, shambling man-shaped creature with radiant blue eyes and a luxurious red-gold-brown pelt. He had a bulbous black nose and a quick, fang-filled smile; he was gentle with those whom he liked and utterly fero-cious toward anyone who provoked him. There were few of his own species to whom Chewbacca was as close as to Han Solo, and the Wookiee was, in turn, Han's only true friend in a very big galaxy.

Gathering his equipment, Chewbacca trudged back out from under the ship.

"Leave that stuff," Han enjoined him. "Sonniod's coming by to say hello." He indicated Sonniod's ship, a light cargo job, parked on her sandskid-mounted landing gear some distance out on the flats. As he had been close to the blast of his plasma torch, Chew-bacca hadn't even heard the landing.

Sonniod, a compact, gray-haired little man with a

cocksure walk and a rakish tilt to his shapeless red bag of a hat, was approaching slowly behind Han. He took in the *Falcon*'s temporary resting place with an amused eye, being a former smuggler and bootlegger. One of the fastest smuggling ships in space, she looked out of place here in the middle of the Kamar Badlands, with little to see in any direction but sand, parched hills, miser-plants, barrel-scrub, and sting-brush. The hot white sun of Kamar was lowering and soon, Sonniod knew, night scavengers would be leaving their burrows and dens. The thought of dig-worms, bloodsniffers, nightswifts, and hunting packs of howlrunners made him shiver a little; Sonniod hated crawly things. He waved and called a greeting to Chewbacca, whom he'd always liked. The Wookiee returned the wave offhandedly, booming a friendly welcome in his own tongue while ascending the ramp to stow his welding equipment and run a test on his repair work.

The *Millennium Falcon* sat on her triangle of landing gear near a natural open-air amphitheater. The encircling slopes showed the prints and tail scuffs left on previous occasions by the Badlanders. Down in the middle of the depression the stubborn plantlife of Kamar had been cleared away. There rested a mass-audience holoprojector, a commercial model that resembled in size and shape a small spacecraft's control console.

"I got word that you wanted a holofeature, any holofeature," Sonniod remarked, following Han down the side of the bowl. *"Love is Waiting* was all I could find on short notice."

"It'll do fine, just fine," Han assured him, fitting the cube into its niche in the projector. "These simple-tons'll watch anything. I've been running the only holo I had, a travelogue, for the past eleven nights. They still keep coming back to gawk at it."

The sun was ready to set and dusk would come

rapidly; this part of the Badlands was close to Kamar's equator. Removing the sweatband he'd been wearing around his forehead, Han bent over the holoprojector. "Everything checks out; we have ourselves a new feature tonight. Come on back to the *Falcon* and I'll let you help me take admission."

Sonniod scowled at having to turn around and climb the bowl again. "I got word on the rumor vine that you were here, but I couldn't understand how in the name of the Original Light you and the Wookiee ended up showing holo to the Kamar Badlanders. Last I heard, you two took some fire on the Rampa Rapids."

Han stopped and scowled at Sonniod. "Who says?"

The little man shrugged elaborately. "A ship looks like a stock freighter but she's leaking a vapor trail on her approach, and the Rampa Skywatch figures she's a water smuggler. They shoot at her when she won't heave to, but she dumps her load, maybe five thousand liters, and cuts deeper into the traffic pattern. What with the thousands of ships landing and lifting off all the time, they never got a positive I.D. on her. And you were seen on Rampa."

Han's eyes narrowed. "Too much chatter can get you into trouble. Didn't your mother ever tell you that, Sonniod?"

Sonniod put on a big grin. "What she told me was never to talk to strangers. And I haven't, not about this, Solo. But I'd have thought you'd have known better. Didn't you check for leakage?"

Han relaxed and shifted his feet. "Next time I'll install the damn tanks myself. That was pure R'alla mineral water, sweet and natural and expensive as hell to haul—worth a fortune on Rampa, where all they've got is that recycled chemical soup. Too bad. Anybody who makes it down the Rampa Rapids with a load of fresh water these days is a rich man."

What Han didn't mention, though he assumed Son-

niod had concluded as much, was that he and Chewbacca had lost all the money they had saved during
those two-and-a-half minutes of fun and excitement
in the Rampa approach corridors.

"As it was, I landed with nothing but the general
cargo I was lugging as cover. And somebody messed
up on that, too! Instead of twelve of the Lockfiller
holo models, I had eleven of them and this old Brosso
Mark II. The consignee would only accept the eleven
Lockfillers and finally wouldn't pay because he'd been
shorted. The shipper liquidated right after I lifted off,
and you know how much I hate police and courts,
so I was stuck with that holoprojector."

"Well, I see you didn't let it put you out of business,
Solo, I'll say that for you," Sonniod granted.

"Inspiration's my specialty," Han agreed. "I knew
it was time to get out of the Corporate Sector for a
while anyway, and I figured the locals out here in
the Badlands would be crazy over holos. I was right;
wait till you see. Oh, and thanks for fronting for
the holo."

"I didn't," Sonniod answered as they resumed their
way. "I know someone who rents them, and *Love is
Waiting* is about the oldest he's got. On my return leg
I'll swap him whatever you've got and pick up a bit
of cash on the side. My cut, all right?"

The deal sounded good to Han.

They returned to the *Falcon,* where a variety of
local trade goods had been heaped at the foot of the
starship's main ramp. As Han and Sonniod arrived, a
labor 'droid came clumping down the ramp bearing a
plastic-extrusion carton containing more Kamarian
wares of various sorts.

The 'droid was somewhat shorter than Han, but
barrel-chested and long-armed, and moved with the
slight stiffness that indicated a heavy-duty suspension
system. It had been designed in the image of man,
with red photoreceptors for eyes and a small vocoder

grille set in his blank metallic face where a mouth would have been. His durable body was finished in a deep, gleaming green.

"How'd you afford a brand-new 'droid?" Sonniod asked as the machine in question set down its burden.

"I didn't," Han answered. "He said they wanted to see the galaxy, but sometimes I think they're both circuit-crazy."

Sonniod looked puzzled. "Both?"

"Watch." The 'droid having completed his chore, Han commanded, "Hey, Bollux, open up."

"Of course, Captain Solo," Bollux answered in a casual drawl, and obligingly pulled his long arms back out of the way. His chest plastron parted down the center with a hiss of pressurized air and the halves swung outward. Nestled among the other elements in his chest was a small, vaguely cubical computer module, an independent machine entity painted a deep blue. A single photoreceptor mounted in a turret at the module's top came alight, swiveled, and came to rest on Han.

"Hello, Captain," piped a childlike voice from a diminutive vocoder grille.

"Well, of all the—" Sonniod exclaimed, leaning closer for a better look as the computer's photoreceptor inspected him up and down.

"That's Blue Max," Han told him. "Max because he's packed to his little eyebrows with computer-probe capacity and Blue for obvious reasons. Some outlaw techs put these two together like that." He thought it best not to go into the wild tangle of crime, conflict, and deception surrounding a previous adventure at the secret Authority installation known as Stars' End.

Bollux's original, ancient body had been all but destroyed there, but the outlaw techs had provided him with a new one. The 'droid had opted for a body much like his old one, insisting that durability, versatility, and the capacity to do useful work had always been the means to his survival. He had even retained his slow speech pattern, having found that it gave him more time to think and made humans regard him as easygoing.

"When they were manumitted they asked to sign on with me," Han told Sonniod. "They're swapping labor for passage."

"Those are the last of the trade articles we've accumulated, sir," Bollux informed Han.

"Good. Close up and go re-stow all the loose gear we had to move around." The plastron halves swished shut on Blue Max, and Bollux obediently returned up the ramp.

"But, Solo, I thought you always said you disavow all machinery that talks back," Sonniod reminded him.

"A little help comes in handy sometimes," Han answered defensively. He avoided further comment, remarking "Ah, the rush is about to start."

Out of the gloom, figures were hurrying toward the starship, pausing at a cautious distance. The Kamar Badlanders were smaller and more supple than other Kamarians, and their segmented exoskeletal chitin was thinner and of a lighter color, matching the hues of their home terrain. Most of them rested in the characteristic pose of their kind, on their lowermost set of extremities and their thick, segmented, prehensile tails.

Lisstik, one of the few Badlanders whom Han could tell from the others, approached the *Falcon*'s ramp. Lisstik had been among the very few to watch the holos on the first evening Han had offered them, and he'd shown up every evening thereafter. He seemed to be a leader among his kind. Now Lisstik was sitting on his tail, leaving his upper two sets of brachia free to gesture and interweave as Kamarians loved to do. The Badlander's faceted, insectile eyes showed no emotion Han had ever been able to read.

Lisstik wore an unusual ornament, a burned-out control integrator that Chewbacca had cast aside. The Kamarian had scavenged and now wore it, bound by a woven band to the front of his gleaming, spherical skull. Lisstik spoke a few phrases of Basic, possibly one of the reasons he was a leader. Once more he asked Han the question that had become something of a formula between them. In a voice filled with clicks and glottal stops, he queried, "Will we see *mak-tk-klp,* your holo-sss, tonight? We have our *q'mai.*"

"Sure, why not?" Han replied. "Just leave the *q'mai* in the usual place and take a—" he almost said "seat," which would have been a difficult concept for a Kamarian, "—a place below. The show starts when everybody's down there."

Lisstik made the common Kamarian affirmative, a clashing-together of the central joints of his upper extremities, sounding like small cymbals. From his side he uncorded a wound scrap of miser-plant leaf and laid it down on a trading tarp Han had spread out at the base of the ramp. Lisstik then scuttled down into the open-air theater with the swift, fluid gait of his species.

Others began to follow, leaving this leaf-wrapped treasure or that handicraft or artwork. Often one Badlander would offer something that constituted the contributions for himself and several companions. Han raised no objection; business was good and there was no reason to push for all the market would bear. He liked to think he was building good will. The Badlanders, who weren't used to congregating, tended to find their places on the slopes in small clusters, keeping as much distance between groups as possible.

Among the payments were water-extraction tubes, pharynx flutes, minutely carved gaming pieces, odd jewelry intended for the exotic Kamarian anatomy, amulets, a digworm opener chipped from glassy stone and nearly as sharp as machined metal, and a delicate prayer necklace. Earlier on, Han had been forced to dissuade his customers from bringing him nightswift gruel, boiled howlrunner, roast stingworm, and other local delicacies.

Han picked up the twist of leaf Lisstik had left, opened it on his palm and showed it to Sonniod. Two small, crude gemstones and a sliver of some milky crystal lay there.

"You'll never get to be a man of leisure at this rate, Solo," opined Sonniod.

Han shrugged, rewrapping the stones. "All I want is a new stake so I can lay in a cargo and get the *Falcon* repaired."

Sonniod studied the starship that had once been, and still looked very much like, a stock light freighter. That she was heavily armed and amazingly speedy was something Han preferred not to have show externally. Such display of force would have been too likely to arouse the curiosity of those entrusted with enforcement of the law.

"She looks spaceworthy enough to me," Sonniod commented. "Same old *Falcon*—looks like a garbage sledge, performs like an interceptor."

"She'll run, now that Chewie's welded the hull," Han conceded, "but some of the control circuitry that was shot up over Rampa was about ready to give up when we got here. Before we came out into the Badlands we had to lay in some new components, and about the only thing you can get here on Kamar is fluidic systems."

Sonniod's face turned sour. "Fluidics? Solo, dear fellow, I'd rather steer my ship with a blunt pole. Why couldn't you get some decent circuitry?"

Han was poring over the rest of his take. "This is a nowhere planet, pal. They've still got nationalism and their weapons—in the advanced places, I mean; not out here in the Badlands—are at the missile-delivered, nuclear-explosive stage. So, of course, someone developed a charged-particle beam to mess up missile circuitry, and naturally everyone turned to fluidics, because shielded circuitry was a little beyond them. So now fluidics is the only type of advanced systems they've got here. We had to load up on adaptor fittings and interface routers and use gas and liquid fluidic components. I *hate* them."

Han stood up again. "I can't stand the thought of all those flow-tracks and microvalves in the *Falcon* and I can't wait to rip 'em out and retool her." He held up and studied with pleasure a statuette carved from black stone, exquisitely detailed and no bigger than his thumb. "And the way things are going, that shouldn't take too much longer."

He put the statuette down in the much smaller of two piles of goods that had been stacked around the starship's ramp. The larger one consisted of trade articles of relatively great bulk and little value, including musical instruments, cooking utensils, tunneling tools, chitin paints, and the portable awnings the Badlanders sometimes used. The smaller pile held all the semiprecious stones, much of the artwork, and a number of the finer tools and implements. The amassed goods had been cluttering up the *Falcon,* stored here and there in available corners of the ship over the past eleven local days. While Chewbacca had been completing repairs that afternoon, Bollux and Han had hauled all the stuff out for sorting and to determine just what it was they had accumulated.

"Maybe not," Sonniod agreed. "Badlanders don't usually trade like this; they're very jealous of their territory. I'm amazed that you've got them flocking together here."

"There's nobody who doesn't enjoy a good show," Han told him. "Especially if they're stuck out in a hole like this place. Or else I wouldn't have all this junk." He watched the last of the stream of Kamarians make their way down and take up their three-point resting positions. "Wonderful customers," he sighed fondly.

"But what'll you do with all the bulky stuff?" Sonniod asked, falling in as Han started down for the center of the amphitheater again.

"We're planning a going-out-of-business sale," Han declared. "Very good deals, everything must go. Super discounts for steady customers and compact items offered in trade." He rubbed his jaw. "I may even sell old Lisstik the holoprojector when I go. I'd hate to see the old Solo Holotheater close down."

"Sentimentalist. So I don't suppose you need work right now?"

Han looked quickly at Sonniod. "What kind of work?"

Sonniod shook his head. "I don't know. Word's out back in the Corporate Sector that there're jobs to be had, runs to be made. Nobody seems to know the details and you never hear names, but word is that if you make yourself available, you'll be contacted."

"I've never worked blind," Han said.

"Nor I. That's why I didn't get in on it. I thought you might be sufficiently hard up to be interested. I must say I'm glad you're not, Solo; it all sounds a bit too tricky. I just thought you might like to know."

Assuring himself of the holoprojector's settings, Han nodded. "Thanks, but don't worry about us; life's a banquet. I might even do this some more, hire out a few projectors and hire local crews on these slowpoke worlds to run them for a split. It could be a sweet, legal little racket, and I wouldn't even have to get shot at."

"By the way," Sonniod said, "what's the other feature, the one you've been showing all along?"

"Oh, that. It's a travelogue, *Varn, World of Water*. You know, life among the amphiboid fishers and ocean farmers in the archipelagoes, deep-sea wildlife, ocean-bed fights to the death between some really big lossors and a pack of cheeb, things like that. Want to hear the narrative? I've got it all memorized."

"Thank you, no," Sonniod replied, pulling his lower lip thoughtfully. "I wonder how they'll react to a new feature?"

"They'll love it," Han insisted. "Singing, dancing; they'll be tapping their little pincers off."

"Solo, what was that word Lisstik used for the admission price?"

"Q'mai." Han was finishing fine adjustments. "They didn't have any word for 'admission,' but I finally got the idea across to Lisstik in spotty Basic and he said the word's *q'mai.* Why?"

"I've heard it before, here on Kamar." Sonniod put the thought aside for the moment. The holofeature appeared in mass-audience projection, filling the air over the natural amphitheater. The Badlanders, who had been swaying gently in the hot night breeze and clicking and chittering among themselves, now became utterly silent.

Love is Waiting was standard fare, Han recalled. It opened without credits or title, which would appear shortly, superimposed on the opening number. That was just as well, Han reflected, since abstract symbols would mean about as much to Kamar Badlanders as particle physics meant to a digworm. He wondered what they would think of human choreography and music, of which there had been none in *Varn, World of Water.*

The feature opened with the woebegone hero stepping off a transporter beltway en route, with some misgiving, to a job with a planetary modification firm. A catchy beat, intended to inform the viewer that a production number was coming, began. Something appeared to make the Badlanders uneasy, however. The clicking and chittering grew louder, nor did it abate when the hero collided with the ingenue and their introduction led to his song cue.

Before the hero had even gotten through the first of his lyrics, discord among the Kamarians was drowning out the music. Several times Han caught the name of Lisstik. He raised the volume a little, hoping the crowd would settle down, puzzling over what had them so agitated.

A stone sailed out of the darkness and bounced off the holoprojector with a crash. From the light spilled by the dancing, singing figures overhead there could be seen the angry waving of Kamarian upper extremities. Multifaceted eyes threw the light back out of the dark in a million fragments.

Another rock clanked against the holoprojector, making Sonniod jump, and a flung howlrunner thighbone, remains of someone's dinner, just missed Han.

"Solo—" began Sonniod, but Han wasn't listening. Having spotted Lisstik, Han shouted up the slopes at him. "Hey, what's going on? Tell 'em to calm down! Give it a chance, will you?"

But it was no use yelling to Lisstik. The Kamarian was surrounded by an irate crowd of his fellows, all waving their upper extremities and thrashing tails, making more noise than Han had ever heard Badlanders make. One of them swiped at the burned-out integrator banded to Lisstik's skull. Elsewhere on the slopes around the holoprojector, shoving, arguments and differences of opinion had erupted into violent disagreement.

"Oh, my," said Sonniod in a very small voice. "Solo, I just remembered what *q'mai* means; I heard it in one of the population centers to the north. It doesn't mean 'admission,' it means 'offering.' Quick, where's the other holo, the travelogue?"

By then a mob of hostile Badlanders was slowly closing in around the holoprojector. Han's hand descended toward his blaster. "Back onboard the *Falcon,* why? What are you talking about?"

"Don't you stop and analyze things, *ever?* You've been showing them holos of a world with more water than they'd ever dreamed existed, filled with cultures and life forms that they've never even fantasized about. You haven't set up a holotheater, you idiot; you've started a *religion!*"

Han gulped, pulling his blaster indecisively as the Badlanders closed in. "Well, how could *I* know? I'm a pilot, not an alien-contact officer!"

He took a handful of Sonniod's coverall sleeve and, pulling gently, led him back slowly toward the *Falcon.* He heard Chewbacca's alarmed roaring from farther up the slope. Overhead, the hero and ingenue and everybody else at the transporter beltway were engaged in a meticulously choreographed dance routine built around the ticket kiosks and turnstiles.

The Badlanders at that side of the circle began to give way uncertainly before Han, who tugged the frightened Sonniod along after him. A number of the bolder Kamarians rushed the holoprojector and began beating at it with sticks, stones, and bare pincers. Overhead, the dance number began to dissolve into distortion. Some of the vandals—or outraged zealots, depending on one's orientation—turned from the projector after a moment and advanced in a vengeful throng on Han.

Sensing correctly that by simply refunding the *q'mai* he stood little chance of mollifying his former audience-cum-congregation, Han fired into the ground before them. Sandy soil exploded, throwing up rocky debris and burning cinders. Whatever flammable material there was in the soil caught fire. Han fired twice more to his right and left, gouging holes in the ground in spectacular bursts.

Badlanders fell back for the moment, their enormous eyes catching the crimson of blaster beams,

ducking their small heads and shielding themselves
with upraised brachia. Han didn't have to fire at the
disgruntled Kamarians between himself and his ship;
they were giving way. "Stay up there," he hollered up
into the darkness at Chewbacca, "and get the engines
started!"

The crowd was doing a pretty fair job of disassem-
bling the holoprojector. Its sound synthesizer was
making simply random noises now, though at high
volume. *Love is Waiting* had devolved to a sluggish
flow of multicolored swirls in the air.

As Han watched, walking backward as calmly as
he could, Lisstik rushed in from the darkness,
wrenched the integrator from his forehead and
hurled it to the ground, stamping and grinding it into
the dust as he beat at the holoprojector with his pincers.

"It looks like your high priest has split with the
church," observed Sonniod. Lisstik succeeded in
wrenching loose a piece of the control panel casing
and flung it in Han's general direction with a vindic-
tive series of clicks.

Feeling himself more the aggrieved party than the
one at fault, Han lost his restraint. "You want a show?
Here's a show, you rotten little ingrate!" He fired into
the holoprojector. The red whining blaster bolt elicited
a brief, bright secondary explosion from somewhere in
the projector's internal reaches.

Suddenly the sound synthesizer was producing the
most appalling string of loud, piercing, unrecogniza-
ble agglutinations of noise Han had ever heard. The
projection filled the sky over the amphitheater with
nova bursts, solar flares, pinwheels, sky rockets, and
strobe flashes. The entire crowd gave a concerted
bleat and charged off in all directions up the slopes
of the bowl.

Han and Sonniod took considerable advantage of
the confusion by sprinting madly toward the *Millen-*

nium Falcon. They could hear harsh chitters and clacks from both sides as Badlanders, having not yet vented their full outrage, began giving chase. Han pegged unaimed shots into the air and the ground behind him. He still hesitated to fire at his former customers unless it meant life or death.

As they neared the *Falcon*'s gaping ramp, Han and Sonniod were gratified to see the starship's belly turret fire a volley. The quad-guns spat lines of red annihilation, and a rocky upcropping already passed by the racing men was transformed into a fountain of sparks, molten rock, and outlashing energy. The heat scorched Han's back and a stone chip whistled past Sonniod's ear, too close for comfort, but it put a halt to the Badlanders' chase for the moment.

When they reached the ramp, Sonniod dashed up at maximum speed while Han slid to a stop on one knee to gather up what he could from the more valuable *q'mai*. A hurled stone bounced off the *Falcon*'s landing gear and another ricocheted from the ramp while Han groped.

"Solo, get up here!" Sonniod screamed. Spinning, Han saw Badlanders closing in around the ship. He fired over their heads and they ducked, but kept coming. Backstepping rapidly up the ramp, Han fired twice more and fell when he dodged a thrown rock. He ended up crawling through the hatch.

As the main hatch rolled down, Chewbacca appeared at the passageway, leaning out of the cockpit with an incensed snarl in his throat.

"How should *I* know what went wrong?" Han bellowed at the Wookiee. "What am I, a telepathist? Get us up and head for Sonniod's ship, *now!*" Chewbacca disappeared back into the cockpit.

As Sonniod helped him up off the deck, Han tried to reassure him. "Don't worry, we'll get you back to your ship before the grievance committee arrives. You'll have time to lift off."

Sonniod nodded thankfully. "But what about you and the Wookiee, Solo?" The starship trembled slightly as she hovered on her thrusters and swung away toward Sonniod's parked vessel. "I wouldn't come back for my profits if I were you."

"I suppose I'll have to head back for the Corporate Sector," Han sighed, "and see what kind of jobs there are floating around. At least the heat should be off; I doubt if anyone's looking for me or this freighter anymore."

Sonniod shook his head. "Try to find out what the job is before you get into it," he encouraged. "Nobody seems to know what kind of run it is."

"I don't care; I'm in no position to be picky. I'll have to take it," Han said, resigned. They heard Chewbacca's dejected hooting drifting aft from the cockpit. "He's right," he said. "We just weren't cut out for the honest life."

II

THE *Millennium Falcon* seemed a ghost ship, a spectral spacecraft like the long-lost, sometimes-sighted *Permondiri Explorer,* or the fabled *Queen of Ranroon.* Trailing sheets of crackling energy, with dancing lines of brilliant discharge playing back and forth over her, she might have flown directly out of one of those legends.

Around the starship seethed the turbulent atmosphere of Lur, a planet quite close, as interstellar distances go, to the Corporate Sector. Its ionization layer was interacting with the *Falcon*'s screens to create eerie lightninglike displays. The shrieking of the planet's winds could be heard through the vessel's hull, and the fury of the storm had cut visibility virtually to zero. Han and Chewbacca paid scant attention to the uproar pounding at their canopy with rain, sleet, snow, and gale-force winds.

They lavished closest attention on their instrumentation, courting it for all the information it could provide, as if by concentration alone they could coax a clearer picture of their situation from sensors and other indicators. Chewbacca growled irritably, his clear blue eyes skipping all over his side of the console, leathery snout working and twitching.

Han was feeling just as cross. "How am *I* supposed to know how thick the ionization layer is? The instrumentation's jittery from the discharges, it doesn't show anything clearly. What do you want me to do,

drop a plumb line?" He went back to closely monitoring his share of the console.

The Wookiee's rejoinder was another growl. Behind him, in the communications officer's seat that
was usually left vacant, Bollux spoke up. "Captain
Solo, one of the indicators just lit up. It appears to be
a malfunction in some of the new control systems."

Without turning from his work, Han uncorked some
of his choicer curses, then calmed down somewhat.
"It's the miserable fluidics! What timing, what *perfect*
timing! Chewie, I told you there'd be trouble, didn't
I? *Didn't I?*"

The Wookiee flailed a huge, hairy paw in the air
by way of dismissal, wishing to be left to his tasks,
rumbling loudly.

"Where's the problem?" Han snapped back over
his right shoulder.

Bollux's photoreceptors scanned the indicators that
were located next to the commo board. "Ship's emergency systems, sir. The auto-firefighting apparatus, I
believe."

"Go back and see what you can do, will you, Bollux? That's all we need, for the firefighting gear to cut
in; we'd be up to our chins in foam and gas before
you could ask the way to the exit." As Bollux staggered off, barely staying upright on the bucking deck,
Han resolutely thrust the problem out of his mind.

Chewbacca yowlped. He had gotten a positive reading. Han dragged himself halfway out of his chair for
a look as another spitting globe of ball-lightning
drifted out and spun off the *Falcon*'s bow mandibles.
The ionization levels were dropping. Then he threw
himself back into his seat and cut the ship's speed
back even further. He had terrible visions of the
ionization level extending down, somehow, to the surface of Lur, blinding them right up to the time of
collision.

Of course, the party who had hired the *Millennium*

Falcon for this run hadn't mentioned the ionization layer, hadn't mentioned anything very specific for that matter. Han had put the word abroad that he and his ship were available for hire and disinclined to ask questions, and the job had come, as Sonniod had predicted it would, from unseen sources in the form of a faceless audio tape and a small cash advance. But with creditors hounding them and their other resources exhausted in the wake of the debacle in the Kamar Badlands, Han and his partner had seen no alternative but to ignore Sonniod's advice and accept the run.

Was I born this stupid, Han asked himself in disgust, *or am I just blossoming late in life?* But at that moment both the storm and the ionization layer parted. The *Falcon* lowered gently through a clear, calm region of Lur's atmosphere. Far below, features of the planet's surface could be seen, mountain peaks protruding through low-hanging, swirling clouds. Another light flashed on; the freighter's long-range sensors had just picked up a landing beacon.

Han switched on the Terrain Following Sensors and poised over the readouts. "They picked us a decent spot to land at least," he admitted. "A big, flat place slung between those two low peaks over there. Probably a glacial field." He flipped the microphone on his headset over to intercom mode. "Bollux, we're going in. Drop what you're doing and hang on."

Correcting his ship's attitude of descent, he brought her in toward the landing point at very moderate speed. The TFS rig showed no obstacles or other dangers, but Han wished to take no chances with instrumentation on this stupid planet.

They settled into the clouds as precipitation was driven at the canopy, only to slide away when it met the *Falcon*'s defensive screens. Sensors had begun functioning normally, giving precise information on altitude. Visibility, even in the storm, was sufficient for a cautious landing. Lur materialized below them as a plain where winds hurried along endlessly, aimlessly.

Han eased the vessel down warily; he had no desire to find himself buried in an ice chasm. But the ship's landing gear found solid support, and instrumentation showed that Han's guess had been correct; they had landed on a glacial ice field. Off to starboard some forty meters or so was the landing beacon.

Han removed his headset, stripped off the flying gloves he had been wearing, and unbuckled his seatbelt. He turned to his Wookiee copilot. "You stay here and keep a sharp watch. I'll go let the ramp down and see what the deal is." The unoccupied navigator's seat behind him held a bundle that he snagged and carried along as he left the cockpit.

On his way aft to the ship's ramp he found Bollux. The 'droid was stooping down by an open inspection plate set in the bulkhead at deck level. Bollux's chest plastron was open, and Blue Max was assisting him in his examination of the problem at hand.

"What's the routine?" Han inquired. "Is it fixed?"

Bollux stood up. "I'm afraid not, Captain Solo. But Max and I caught it just before the last safety went. We shut down the entire system, but repair is beyond the capability of either of us."

"You don't need a tech for those fluidics, Captain," Max chirped. "You need a damn *plumber*." His voice held a note of moral outrage at the inferior design.

"Tell me about it. And watch your language, Max. Just because I talk that way is no sign you should. All right, boys, just leave things the way they are. This trip should make us enough to have all those waterworks replaced with good old shielded circuitry. Bollux, I want you to close up your fruit stand; we've got cargo to pick up and I don't want you making the clients jumpy. Sorry, Max, but you do that to people sometimes."

"No problem, Captain," Blue Max replied as the halves of Bollux's chest swung shut to the hum of servomotors. Han reflected that, while he still didn't care much for automata, Bollux and Max weren't too bad. He decided, though, that he would never understand how the pseudo-personalities of an ancient labor 'droid and a precocious computer module could hit it off so well.

Han opened the bundle he had brought from the cockpit—a bulky thermosuit—and began pulling it on over his ship's clothes. Before fitting his hands into the thermosuit's attached gloves, he adjusted his gunbelt, rebuckling it over the suit, then removing the weapon's trigger guard so that he'd be able to fire it with his thermoglove on. He wouldn't have dreamed of going out unarmed; he was always wary when the *Millennium Falcon* was grounded in unfamiliar surroundings, but especially so when he was doing business on the shady side of the street.

He donned protective headgear, a transparent facebowl with insulated ear cups. Touching a button on the control unit set in his thermosuit's sleeve, he brought its heating unit to life.

"Stand by," he ordered Bollux, "in case I need a hand with the cargo."

"May I inquire what it is we're to carry, Captain?" Bollux asked as he drew aside the covers of the special compartments hidden under the deckplates.

"You may guess, Bollux; that's about all I can do right now myself." Han prodded at the hatch control with a gloved finger. "Nobody mentioned what it's going to be, and I was in no position to ask. Couldn't be anything too massive, I guess."

The hatch rolled up and a blast of frigid wind invaded the passageway. Han shouted over the wail of the storm. "Doesn't look like it's going to be heat rash salve though, does it?"

He started down the ramp, leaning into the force

of the gale. The cold in his lungs was sharp enough
to make him think about going back for a respirator,
but he judged that he wouldn't be outside long enough
to need one. His facebowl polarized somewhat against
the ice glare as snow hissed against it. Specific gravity
here on Lur was slightly over Standard, but not
enough to cause any inconvenience.

At the foot of the ramp he found that the wind was
moving a light dusting of snow across the blue-
white glacier. Miniature drifts were already accumu-
lating against the *Falcon*'s landing gear. He spied the
beacon, a cluster of blinking caution lights atop a
globular transponder package, anchored to glacial ice
by a tripod. There was no one to be seen, but visibility
was so low that Han couldn't have made out much
beyond the landing marker.

He walked over to it, inspecting it and finding it to
be nothing more than a standard model, designed for
use in places lacking sophisticated navigational and
tracking equipment.

Suddenly a muffled voice behind him called out.
"Solo?" He spun, right hand dropping automatically
to the grip of his blaster. A man stepped out of the
swirl of the storm. He, too, wore a thermosuit and a
facebowl that had muted his voice, but the thermosuit
was white and the facebowl reflective, making him
nearly invisible there on the glacier.

He moved forward with hands empty and held
high. Han, squinting past him, saw the vague outlines
of other figures moving just at the edge of his range
of vision.

"I'm him," Han responded, his own words muffled
somewhat by his facebowl. "You're, uh, Zlarb?"

The other nodded. Zlarb was a tall, broadly built
man with extremely fair skin, white-blond beard
and clear gray eyes with creases at their corners that
gave him an intense, threatening look. But he showed

his teeth in a wide smile. "That's right, Captain. And I'm ready to go, too. We can load up right away."

Han tried to peer through the curtain of snow behind Zlarb. "Are there enough of you to bring up the cargo? I brought along a repulsorlift handtruck in case you need it to haul your load. Want me to run it out for you?"

Zlarb gave him a look Han couldn't quite read, then smiled again. "No. I think we can get our shipment onboard without any problems."

Something about the man's behavior, the hint of a private joke or the sardonic tone to his reply, made Han suspicious. He had long since learned to listen to inner alarms. He looked back at the blurry outline of the *Falcon* and hoped Chewbacca was alert and that the Wookiee had the starship's main batteries primed and aimed. The two seldom encountered trouble from their pickup contacts. Usually at the other end, the drop-off and payment end of things, trouble tended to occur. But this just might be the exception.

Han backed away a step, eyes meeting Zlarb's. "All right then, I'll go get ready to raise ship." He had more questions to ask this man, but wanted to move the proceedings to a more auspicious spot, say, next to the freighter's belly turrret. "You drag your shipment to the ramp head and we'll take it from there."

Zlarb's grin was wider now. "No, Solo. I think we'll both go onboard your ship. Right now."

Han was about to tell Zlarb that it was against his and Chewbacca's policy to let smuggling contacts onboard when he noticed that the man had turned his hand over. In it he held a tiny weapon, a short-range palmgun that, like a conjuror, he must have held hidden between gloved fingers. Han thought about going for his blaster but realized that at best he could probably manage no more than a tie, in which case both of them would die.

The blinking lights of the landing beacon, gleaming off Zlarb's facebowl, gave the man's smirk an even more sinister look. "Hand the blaster over butt-first, Solo, and keep your back to the ship so your partner can't see. Carefully now; I've been warned about you and that speeddraw, and I'd rather shoot than take a chance."

He tucked Han's sidearm into his belt. "Now let's get aboard. Keep both hands at your sides and don't try to warn the Wookiee."

He turned for a moment and motioned to unseen companions, then indicated the *Falcon* with the palmgun. From a distance, Han thought, it probably looked like a polite you-first gesture.

As they walked Han tried to sort through the situation, his mind roiling. These people knew exactly what they were doing; the whole job had been a setup. Zlarb's frank willingness to use his weapon was proof that he and his accomplices were playing for very high stakes. The question of being cheated of payment or even of having his vessel hijacked suddenly bothered Han less than the thought of not surviving the encounter.

The bulk of the *Millennium Falcon* became more distinct as they approached her. "No bright stunts now, Solo," Zlarb warned. "Don't even twitch your nose at the Wookiee or you'll die for it."

Han had to admit that Zlarb thought in advance, but he hadn't covered everything. Han and Chewbacca had a signal system for pickups and dropoffs, whereby Han didn't need to communicate that something was wrong; all he had to do was approach the ship and fail to give the subtle all's-well.

Over the moan of the gale they heard the whine of servomotors. The quad-guns in the *Falcon*'s belly turret traversed, elevated, and came to bear on them.

But Zlarb had already stepped behind Han, pulling the captured gun from his belt and holding its muzzle up close to Han's temple. They could see Chewbacca now, his hairy face pressed close to the canopy, gazing down apprehensively. The Wookiee's left arm was stretched behind him, down near the console. Han knew his friend's fingers would be only millimeters from the fire controls. He wanted to yell *Get out! Raise ship!* But Zlarb anticipated that. "Not a word to him, Solo! Not a sound, or you're canceled." Han didn't doubt him a bit.

Zlarb had the Wookiee's attention and was motioning him to come down out of the ship, indicating with the blaster's muzzle just what would happen to Han if Chewbacca failed to obey. Han, familiar with his shaggy first mate's expressions, read indecision, then resignation, on his face. Then the Wookiee disappeared from the cockpit.

Han muttered something, and Zlarb poked him with the blaster. "Save it; it's lucky for you he paid attention. Just play along and both of you will come through this alive."

Two of Zlarb's underlings had come up and stopped near their boss. One was a human, a squat, tough looking ugly who could have come from any of 100,000 worlds. The other was a humanoid, a giant, burly creature nearly Chewbacca's size, with tiny eyes beneath jutting, boney brows. The humanoid's skin was a glossy brown, like some exotic, polished wood, and vestigial horns curled at his forehead. He seemed to feel the need for neither thermosuit nor facebowl.

But it was what the other man, the squat one, had brought that surprised Han most. He had a control leash fastened to his wrist; at the end of the leash was a nashtah, one of the storied hunting beasts of Dra III. The nashtah's six powerful legs, each armed with long, curving, diamond-hard claws, shifted restlessly on the ice. It strained at its leash, tongue arcing, its steamy breath rasping between triple rows of jagged white teeth, its long barbed tail lashing. Its muscles,

tensing and untensing, sent ripples along its green,
sleek hide.

*What in the name of the profit-motive system can
they be doing with a nashtah?* Han asked himself.
The creatures were bloodthirsty, tireless and impossible to shake once they scented their prey, and were
among the most vicious of all attack animals. That
seemed to indicate poaching of some kind, but why
would a gang of poachers go to all this trouble? Han
disliked moving pelts or hides and, given a choice,
would not have carried them. But that surely didn't
call for this kind of extreme action on Zlarb's part;
there were plenty of smugglers who would have taken
the job.

Chewbacca appeared at the ramp head. The
nashtah, sighting him, gave throat to a piercing
scream and lunged, dragging its handler until he dug
in his heels and pressed a stud on the control leash
handle. The nashtah gave a yeowl of displeasure at
the mild shock that stopped its advance for the moment. Chewbacca watched impassively, his bowcaster
held ready, eyes sweeping the scene below.

Zlarb started Han off with a shove, staying close
behind, and the two climbed the ramp. When they
were near the top, Zlarb addressed Chewbacca. "Put
down the weapon. Do it now and step back or your
friend here gets fried." There was the nudge of the
blaster between Han's shoulder blades.

Chewbacca debated the variables involved, then
complied, seeing no other way to save his friend's
life. Meanwhile, Han evaluated his chances for a fast
move. He knew he might stand a chance of neutraliz-
ing Zlarb, but the other two gang members were backing their boss up and each had a handgun out now.
And then there was the nashtah. Han elected to post-
pone his most desperate option for the time being.

When they reached the top of the ramp, Zlarb
pushed Han hard, then stooped to take up Chew-

bacca's bowcaster. The Wookiee caught his friend as
Han stumbled from the shove and kept him from
falling. Han removed his facebowl and threw it aside.
Taking a quick look around, he noticed Bollux still
standing where Han had left him. The 'droid seemed
to be rooted to the spot, immobile with surprise, his
circuitry struggling to absorb the bewildering rush of
events.

Zlarb's men had come in behind him along with the
nashtah, whose claws scraped the deckplates. Again it
had to be curbed from leaping at the Wookiee, and
Han wondered for a moment what it was about
Chewbacca that antagonized it so. Something about
his first mate's scent, or perhaps a resemblance to one
of the beast's natural enemies?

Zlarb turned to the hulking humanoid who had
been eyeing Chewbacca with nearly as much hostility
as the nashtah. "Go tell the others to start moving.
We'll get things ready here." Then he turned to Han.
"Open up your main hold; we're going to start loading." And finally, to the handler who still restrained
the spitting nashtah, Zlarb indicated the Wookiee.
"If he moves, burn him down."

They set off aft, Zlarb being careful to stay well
back from Han, watchful for any surprise move the
pilot might make. Following the curve of the passageway, they came to the hatchway of the *Falcon*'s main
cargo hold. Han tapped the release, and the hatch
slid back to reveal a compartment of modest size,
ribbed by the ship's structural members, featureless
except for air ducts, safety equipment, and the
heating-refrigeration unit. A stack of panels and dis-
assembled support posts lay there, to be erected as
shelving or retaining bins if they were needed. Dun-
nage and padding were heaped in a pile to one side
near coils of strapping and fastening tackle.

Zlarb, looking around, nodded in approval. "This'll

do fine, Solo. Leave the hatch open and let's get back to the others."

Another of Zlarb's men had arrived and was standing at the top of the ramp, a disruptor rifle leveled at Chewbacca. The nashtah handler had dragged his beast back farther toward the cockpit. The big humanoid had returned, too, carrying a small shoulder pack. Zlarb pointed to it. "You've got your equipment there, Wadda?"

Wadda inclined his head. Zlarb pointed to Bollux. "First I want you to stick a restraining bolt on the 'droid. We don't want him wandering around; he might give us trouble."

Bollux started to protest but weapons moved to cover him and Wadda closed in on him, looming over him and unlimbering the ominous pack from his shoulder. The labor 'droid's red photoreceptors went to Han in what seemed to be an entreaty. "Captain Solo, what shall I—"

"Keep still," Han instructed, not wanting to see Bollux destroyed and knowing Zlarb's people would do just that if the 'droid resisted them. "It'll only be for a while."

Bollux looked from Han to Chewbacca, then to Wadda and back to Han again. Wadda closed in on him, fitting a restraining bolt into a hand-held applicator. The big humanoid pressed the applicator against Bollux's chest and the 'droid gave a split-second bleep. There was a wisp of smoke as bolt fused to metal skin. Just as Bollux shuffled, resettling his clanging feet as if some new posture would be of help to him, his photoreceptors went dark, the restraining bolt deactivating his control matrices.

Satisfied that the *Falcon* was his, Zlarb began issuing commands. "Let's get busy." Han was directed to Chewbacca's side. The nashtah handler and the man with the disruptor rifle continued to watch them while

Wadda hurried down the ramp, making it tremble under his great weight.

"Zlarb," Han began, "don't you think it's time you told us what's so flaming . . ."

He was distracted by the ramp's vibrations and the sound of many light footfalls. A moment later he understood just what had happened to him and in how dangerous a situation he and Chewbacca had become involved.

A file of small figures trooped aboard, heads hung in fatigue and despair. These were obviously inhabitants of Lur. The tallest of them was scarcely waist-high to Han. They were erect bipeds, covered with fine white fur, their feet protected by thick pads of calluslike tissue. Their eyes were large, and ran toward green and blue; they stared around the *Falcon*'s interior in dull amazement.

Each neck was encircled by a collar of metal, the collars joined together by a thin black cable. It was a slaver's line.

Chewbacca bellowed an enraged roar and ignored the answering scream from the nashtah. Han glared at Zlarb, who was directing the loading of slaves. One of his men held a director unit, its circuitry linked to the collars. The director, a banned device, had an unfinished, homemade look to it. Any defiance from the captives would earn them excruciating pain.

Han fixed Zlarb with his eye. "Not in my ship," he stated, emphasizing each word.

But Zlarb only laughed. "You're not in much of a position to object, are you, Solo?"

"Not in my ship," Han repeated stubbornly. "Not slaves. Never."

Zlarb aligned Han's own blaster at him, sighting down the barrel. "You just think again, pilot. If you give me any trouble, you'll end up locked in a necklace yourself. Now, you and the Wookiee go forward and get ready to lift."

A second line of slaves was being led aboard and ushered aft to the hold. Han scowled at Zlarb for a moment, then turned toward the cockpit. Chewbacca hesitated, bared his fangs at the slavers once more, and followed his friend.

Han lowered himself unwillingly into the pilot's seat, and Chewbacca took the copilot's. Zlarb stood behind them watching their every move carefully. He mistrusted the two, of course, but knew that they could get more speed and better performance out of the *Falcon* than he or any of his men could. And that might well mean survival in the perilous business of slave-running.

"Solo, I want you and your partner to be smart about this. You take us to our point of delivery and you'll both be taken care of. But if we're halted and boarded, it's the death sentence for all of us, you included."

"Where are we going?" Han asked, tight-lipped.

"I'll tell you that when the time comes. For now, you just prepare to raise ship."

Han brought the *Falcon*'s engines to full power, warming up her shields and preparing to lift. "What are they paying you? Even *I* can't think of enough money to get me mixed up in slaving."

Zlarb chuckled derisively. "They told me you were a hard case, Solo. I see they were wrong. Those little beauties back there are worth four, five, maybe even six thousand apiece on the Invisible Market. They're natural-born experts at genetic manipulation, and in great demand, my friend. Not everyone is happy with the rigid restrictions that were imposed after the Clone Wars. It seems these creatures like their own world too much, though, and wouldn't sign out on contract labor for anything. So my associates and I rounded up a bunch. A few of them are sick or wounded, but we'll deliver at least fifty of them. I'll make enough off this run to keep me happy and lazy for a long time."

Contract labor. That sounded like the Corporate Sector Authority was involved. But though the Authority had been known to use contract hoaxes and deceptive recruitment, Han found it hard to believe that it would be so bold as to practice out-and-out slavery, particularly raiding a planet outside its own boundaries. That was something even the Empire couldn't afford to ignore.

"Your board looks good to me, Solo," Zlarb commented, studying the console. "Raise ship."

As Han, Chewbacca, and the slavers left the passageway, Bollux still stood precisely where he had been deactivated near the ramp's head. The restraining bolt had interdicted all his control centers, immobilizing him.

But hidden within the labor 'droid's thorax, still functioning off his own independent power supply, Blue Max was assessing his situation. Though he realized that the emergency might mean disaster for the *Falcon*'s entire complement, the undersized computer probe could see little he could do to change the situation. He had no motor capability of his own and contained no communications equipment except his vocoder and various computer-tap adaptors. Moreover, Max's own power source was miniscule in comparison to Bollux's, and he couldn't possibly move the labor 'droid's body far enough or fast enough to do any good before exhausting himself.

Blue Max wished he could at least talk to his friend, but the restraining bolt's interdiction extended to all of Bollux's brain functions. The computer, who had seldom been separated from Bollux's host body, felt very much alone.

Then he remembered the short bleep emitted by Bollux just before he'd been immobilized. Max ran the bleep back, slowing it by a high factor and finding, as he had thought, that it was a squirt, a burst transmission. It was garbled; Bollux had been dealing with a number of things at the time. But at length Max made sense of it and saw what the labor 'droid had been trying to do.

Blue Max linked himself in carefully with some of Bollux's motor circuitry, prepared to withdraw and close off instantly if the bolt's influence threatened to impair him.

But it didn't. The restraining bolt worked against Bollux's command and control centers, not his actual circuitry and servomotors. Still, Max knew he had a very difficult task, one that would have been impossible if Bollux hadn't repositioned his feet at the last instant before being paralyzed.

The computer lacked the power to make Bollux's body take more than a few steps but he did have enough to effect a single servo. Though it drained him dangerously, Max fed all the power he could into the knee joint of his companion's left leg. The knee flexed and the labor 'droid's body tilted. Max, trying desperately to gauge the unfamiliar leverages and angles, stopped for a moment and redirected his efforts toward the central torsion hookup in Bollux's midsection, turning him a little to the left. That demanded so much of his scant power that Max had to pause for a moment and let his reserves build a bit.

He shut down all nonvital parts of himself to hoard the energy he needed, then addressed himself to the knee joint once more as the roar of the *Millennium Falcon*'s warming engines made the deckplates chatter and filled the passageway with a hollow rumble.

The 'droid's balance passed the critical point; he tottered, then toppled to the left, landing with a clamorous din. Bollux's body ended up resting on its left arm and side, barely stablilized by its right foot, which also touched the deck.

Max found that, with the body in this position, he couldn't get both chest panels open, but that hardly mattered since he lacked the power to do so anyway. As it was, he had to stop twice in working the right panel outward, wait for his reserves to build up, then channel power into the panel servo. He stopped when the right panel was open sufficiently for him to see his objective.

The last move was the hardest. Max extended an adaptor to the exposed fluidics systems on which he and Bollux had been working prior to planetfall. The fluidics were fitted with standard couplings, but that still left the problem of making a connection with them. Extending his rodlike adaptor arm as far as it would go, Max found his goal just out of reach. The coupling waited beyond and below his adaptor. In desperation Max tried to push his adaptor arm out even farther and nearly damaged himself. It availed nothing.

The computer saw he had only one chance left. That it involved risk of personal damage to him didn't make him hesitate for an instant. He shifted power back to Bollux's midsection, turning the torsion hookup again in an all-out effort that nearly overloaded him. The labor 'droid's body twisted slowly, then rolled over.

But in the last moment, the roll brought Max's adaptor close enough to make contact with the fluidics coupling. He linked up with the systems and had time to send out a single command. Then the torso's descending weight bent his fragile adaptor arm, breaking the connection, and sending feedback washing into Blue Max with a computer analogue of blinding pain.

While Max fought his lonely battle, Han was staring at his controls. He was perspiring and had the front of his thermosuit open, wondering if he should let things go any further or try to jump Zlarb now.

Zlarb was scanning the control console. "I told you to get going, Solo. Raise ship."

He was still waving Han's blaster around to emphasize his command when he took a gush of thick, white foam full in the face.

Nozzles in the cockpit and throughout the *Millennium Falcon* had begun to spew anti-incendiary gas and suppression foam when Max's single command cut in the ship's auto-firefighting apparatus. Under the computer probe's override, the system behaved as if the entire ship were aflame.

Han and Chewbacca, unsure of what was happening, didn't stop to think, but seized instead upon whatever freak opportunity this was. The Wookiee struck out with a huge paw, backhanding Zlarb against the navigator's seat, located just behind Han's. Zlarb, blinded, let off a shot at random. The blaster blew a jagged hole in the canopy, its edges dripping with molten transparisteel.

Just then Han flung himself on the slaver, followed closely thereafter by his first mate. Zlarb was punched, shaken, kneed, bitten, and slammed head-first into the navi-computer before he could get off a second shot.

The cockpit was already ankle-deep in foam, and blasts of anti-incendiary gas made it nearly impossible to see. The racket of sirens and warning hooters was deafening. Nevertheless, both partners' spirits had risen appreciably. Picking up his blaster, Han cupped his hand to his mouth and hollered into Chewbacca's ear.

"I don't know what's going on, but we've got to hit them before they can recover. I counted six of them, right?"

The Wookiee confirmed the number. Han led the way from the cockpit as quickly as he could, both of them slipping and sliding in the deepening foam.

Han dashed out into the main passageway. Fortunately he looked to his right first, toward the forward compartment. There one of the slavers stood open-mouthed, staring at the belching auto-firefighting gear. He caught sight of Han and started to bring his disruptor rifle around. But Han's blaster bolt took him high in the chest, knocking him backward through the air, his weapon dropping from his hands.

Han heard a horrible growl and whirled. The handler appeared from the other direction and released the nashtah, which sprang at Han with such speed that it was no more than a blur. Before he could even get off a shot the beast hit him, sending him sprawling against the squares of safety cushioning that rimmed the cockpit hatchway, his shoulder and one forearm slashed with parallel furrows from the creature's claws.

But the nashtah never completed its pounce. Instead it was grabbed and held in midair and sent hurtling against a bulkhead. Chewbacca, having lost his footing in the act of throwing the nashtah aside, scrambled to his feet once more. Han brought his gun up but hesitated to shoot because the fall had shaken him. In that moment the nashtah, with an angry flick of its tail and a hideous cry, sprang at the Wookiee, driving him back into the cockpit passageway.

Chewbacca somehow managed to maintain his footing. Exerting to the fullest his astounding strength, he absorbed the force of the nashtah's attack, locking his hairy hands around its throat, hunching his shoulders and working with legs and forearms to ward off its claws.

The nashtah screamed again, and the Wookiee screamed even louder. Chewbacca held the attack beast clear of the deck and slammed it against the bulkhead to his left, then to his right and to the left again, all in less than a second. The nashtah, its head dangling now at a very odd angle, slumped in his grasp. Chewbacca let it fall to the deck.

The beast's handler gave an outraged shout, seeing

his animal's unmoving body. He brought his pistol up, but Han's blaster reacted first. The man staggered, tried to bring his weapon up again, and Han fired a second time. The handler fell prone on the deck not far from the body of his nashtah.

Han grabbed Chewbacca's elbow, pointed and started aft toward the main hold. They found Bollux's inert bulk where Blue Max had caused it to fall, and it was apparent just what the two automata had done. Foam had crept in around the 'droid's body and had begun seeping in through the open chest panel.

Chewbacca gave a grating snarl alluding to the ingenuity of the two. "I'll second that; they're pretty nervy," Han concurred. He'd taken a grip on the 'droid's shoulder. "Help me sit him up so the foam doesn't get at them."

There was no time to do anything else. They propped the 'droid's body against the bulkhead in temporary safety and hurried on. They were going full-tilt when the giant humanoid appeared around the curve of the passageway from the opposite direction, a riot gun in his hand.

Han made an awkward attempt to dodge for cover, bringing his blaster up at the same time. With the deck slippery with foam, he lost his footing and took a spill. Chewbacca, on the other hand, adapted quickly to these unusual conditions. Without decreasing speed he hurled himself into a feet-first slide along the deckplates, cutting a bow-wave through the drifting foam, his enthusiastic bellow rising above the hiss of gas projectors and the alarms.

The slaver's aim wavered from Han to the Wookiee, but Chewbacca was moving too fast; one shot mewed, a miss that crackled on the deck, raising steam from the foam. The Wookiee rammed the humanoid with his outsized feet, and the humanoid bounced with astonishing abruptness into a mound of foam wherein he was joined directly by Chewbacca. The foam mound quivered and shook, strands and clumps of it flying loose, as there came from it the sounds of snarls and roars, and heavyweight collision.

Han was back on his feet, rushing on, feeling somewhat lightheaded from the anti-incendiary gas. He was still uncertain what to do when he encountered the last two slavers, the ones carrying the collar-boxes. If he hesitated they might just hit the kill switches, slaying every captive on the lines. He steeled himself to fire accurately and without an instant's delay.

But the responsibility wasn't his. The main hold was in pandemonium. Both remaining slavers were staggering under swarming, flailing captives. All the creatures moved with agonized, twitching motions, fighting both their captors and the pulses of excruciating pain being inflicted by their collars. Many were on the deck, unable to overcome the punishment and join the fight.

But those who had mastered their agony were carrying the battle well. As Han watched, they dragged the slavers to the deck, wresting away weapons and director units and pounding the two into submission. Apparently the creatures knew enough about the director units to deactivate them. All the slaves slumped visibly as their torture ended.

Han stepped cautiously into the hold. He hoped his unwilling passengers understood the situation well enough to know that he wasn't their enemy, but reminded himself to better be charming until they were sure.

One of the creatures, its thick white fur ruffled and tufted from its struggle, was studying the collarbox. It made a decisive stab at a switch and all the collars along that particular cable sprang open. The creature tossed the director unit aside contemptuously, and one of its companions passed it a captured disruptor. The sidearm looked big and clumsy in its small, nimble hands.

Han holstered his blaster slowly, holding empty palms up for them all to see. "I didn't want this either," he told them in an even tone, though he doubted that they spoke a shared language. "I had no more to do with it than you."

The disruptor was moving slowly. Han argued with himself the wisdom of reaching for his pistol but doubted his own ability to shoot the creature down. It had no fault in this matter either. He decided to reason on, but the skin of his neck was trying to crawl up into his scalp.

"Listen: you're free to go. I'm not going to stop—"

He sprang sideways as the disruptor swung up at him. It took an iron, conscious effort to keep from drawing. He heard the disruptor's blaring report. And unexpectedly, he heard a small clatter and a gasp from behind him.

Framed in the hatchway, looking down without comprehension at the broad wound in his chest, was Zlarb. At his feet lay the little palmgun. He sank against the hatchway and slid slowly to the deck. The creature had lowered its disruptor once more. Han went and knelt by Zlarb.

The slaver was breathing very unevenly between clenched teeth, his eyes screwed shut. He opened them then, focusing on Han, who had been about to tell him to save his strength, but saw that it made no difference. Perhaps, in a full-facility medicenter, the slaver could have been saved, but with the limited resources of the *Falcon*'s medipacks Zlarb was as good as gone.

He didn't avoid the slaver's gaze. "They weren't quite as meek as you thought, were they Zlarb?" he asked quietly. "Just real, real patient."

Zlarb's eyes began to flutter shut again. He only managed "Solo . . ." He put more hatred into the name than Han would have thought possible.

"And how did Zlarb get past you? He almost scored me, you big slug!"

Chewbacca gobbled angrily in response to Han's indignant question and pointed to where the burly humanoid slaver, the one with whom the Wookiee had collided, lay battered and bound by the main ramp.

"So what?" Han demanded with elaborate sarcasm, enjoying himself. He was kneeling by Bollux's side, setting the cup of an extractor over the restraining bolt. "You used to handle three of his kind before breakfast. What I *don't* need is a first mate who's turning into a geriatric case."

Chewbacca barked so loudly that Han ducked involuntarily. A Wookiee's lifespan is longer than a human's—age was a standing joke between the two.

"That's what *you* say." Han thumbed the extractor's switch. There was a pop and a tiny burst of blue discharge around the bolt's base.

Bollux's red photoreceptors came on. "Why, Captain Solo! Thank you, sir. Does this mean the crisis has passed?"

"All but the housework. I got the firefighting outlets shut down, but the ship looks like an explosion in a dessert shop. You can skate from here to the cockpit if you want. That was a good move you and Maxie—"

"Blue Max!" Bollux interrupted, a rarity for him. "Sir, he's not in linkage; I think he's been damaged."

"We know. His adaptor arm was bent and he took some burnout creepage. Chewie says he can fix him up, though, with components we have onboard. Just leave Max be for now. Can you get up?"

The labor 'droid answered by rising and swinging his chest panel shut over the computer module protectively. "Blue Max is remarkably resourceful, wouldn't you say, Captain?"

"Bet your anodes. If he had fingers we'd have to start locking up the tableware. You can tell him that

for me later, but for now just take it easy." Han stood
and beckoned Chewbacca and the two went aft to the
hold again.

The former captives had laid out the bodies of their
several dead, those who hadn't survived the terrible
ordeal of the slave collars. They were assembling lit-
ters from materials in the hold, which Han had offered
them, with which to bear their fellows home.

Han stopped by the corpse of Zlarb. In searching the
man a few minutes earlier, he had noticed the hard,
rectangular lump of a breast-pocket security case under his thermosuit. Han had seen a few such cases
before and knew he had to be careful with it.

Settling down with one of the *Falcon*'s medipacks, he
dug out a flexclamp and a vibroscalpel and began
cutting away the tough material of the thermosuit. In
the meantime, Chewbacca began cleaning his own
wounds with an irrigation bulb and a synthflesh dispenser. More by fortune than design, neither of the
two had received deep wounds from the nashtah's
claws.

Han quickly had the security case exposed. It was
anchored to the pocket by a slim clip to which it was
attached by a fine wire. Han carefully felt for and
found the safety, a small button concealed at the
case's lower edge. Pressing it, he disengaged the security circuit. Then he began working the clip loose from
the pocket lining with his other hand. To try to remove
the case in any other fashion would invite a neuro-
paralysis charge from the case. A numb arm would be
the best he could hope for, depending on the case's
setting. Some security cases were capable of giving lethal shocks.

He reprimed the clip, and the case was rendered
harmless. Humming a half-remembered tune, he got
busy with some fine-work instruments he had fetched
from the ship's small but complete tool locker. The
lock itself was a fairly common model; the neuro-

shock was the case's main line of defense. He had it
open in fairly short order.

And spat some sizzling Corellian oaths. There was no
money.

All the case contained were a data plaque, a message tape, and smaller case that turned out to be a
Malkite poisoner's kit. That Zlarb was a practitioner
of the Malkite poisoner's arts reaffirmed Han's conviction that the universe wouldn't mourn the man's
passing, but it did little to alleviate his frustration or
his financial situation.

He threw aside the security case and glowered at the
two surviving human slavers. They both began to quake
visibly. "You have one chance," he said quietly.
"Somebody owes me money; I have ten thousand
credits coming for this run and I want it. Not telling
me where I can get it would be the dumbest thing
you'll ever do in your lives, and one of the very last."

"We don't know anything, Solo, we swear," one of
them protested. "Zlarb hired us on and he arranged
everything; he handled the contacts and all the
money himself. We never saw anybody else, that's
the truth." His comrade confirmed it energetically.

The ex-slaves had finished their preparations and
were ready to depart. Han walked over to where the
empty collars and director units lay. "That's really rotten luck for you two," he told the slavers and fastened
a collar around the neck of each, ignoring their protests. He handed the collar-box to the leader of the
ex-slaves and pointed to the bodies of the dead.

The creature understood, patting the case. The
slavers would pay for the deaths with their own servitude. How long a sentence they'd have to serve would
be entirely up to their one-time captives. Han couldn't
have cared less.

"Take your boss's body with you," he ordered the
two. They looked at one another. The creature's finger poised near the controls of their collars. They

scrambled to obey, hoisting the late Zlarb between them.

Chewbacca led the way as the ex-slaves, preceded by their new servants, bore their dead from the cargo hold. "Don't forget to get rid of the other casualties," Han called after his friend. "And collar up that other slaver for them. Then bring me a reader!"

Exhausted, he resolutely set to the task of cleaning up his injuries with another irrigation bulb, thinking ominous thoughts about how little money he and Chewbacca had left and wondering if their rotten luck would ever break. Then it occurred to him that Zlarb would undoubtedly have killed him, and Chewbacca as well, if Blue Max and Bollux hadn't given the situation a twist. As it was, he and the Wookiee were alive and free and, with a little cleaning up, would have their starship in something like running order again very shortly. By the time Chewbacca returned, Han was applying synthflesh to his wounds and whistling to himself.

The Wookiee was carrying a portable readout. Han shoved the medipack aside and fit the data plaque into the reader. His copilot leaned over his shoulder and together they puzzled over what they saw.

"Date-time coordinates, planetary index numbers," Han muttered. "Ships' registry codes and rental agents' IDs. Most of them for a planet called Ammuud." Chewbacca rumbled his own mystification.

Han again cursed Zlarb. Removing the plaque, he inserted the message tape into the readout's other aperture. On the screen appeared the face of a young, black-haired man. The tight closeup told Han nothing about the man's surroundings, whereabouts, or even the clothing he wore.

The face in the portable readout began speaking. "The measures you suggested are being taken against the Mor Glayyd on Ammuud. When delivery of your current consignment is made, payment will take place

on Bonadan. Be at table 131, main passenger lounge,
Bonadan Spaceport Southeast II at these coordinates."
Standard date-time coordinates appeared on the
screen for a moment, then it cleared.

Han tossed the reader into the air with a burst of
laughter. "If we pour it on, we can still get there in
time. Let's get the canopy patched; we can tidy up
and see to Bollux and Max while we're in jump."

He kissed the reader and the Wookiee brayed,
muzzle wrinkling, tongue curling, fangs showing. It
was time to see about payments due.

III

HAN Solo was obliged to raise his voice to deliver the punch line. A gargantuan ore barge was settling in with such a booming of brute engines that, even though it was grounding halfway across the vast spaceport, it set up tiny wavelets in drinks in the passenger terminal's main lounge.

The main lounge of Bonadan Spaceport Southeast II was colossal and, besides the unceasing rumble of arriving and departing ships, was filled with the conversation of thousands of human and nonhuman customers that overtaxed its sound-muting system. The lounge's transparent dome revealed a sky teeming with ships of every description, their comings and goings orchestrated by the most advanced control system available. Planetary and solar system shuttles, passenger liners, the enormous barges carrying food and raw materials, Authority Security Police fleet ships, and bulk freighters bearing away Bonadan's manufactured goods—all combined to make this one of the busiest ports in the Corporate Sector.

Although it encompassed tens of thousands of star systems, the Corporate Sector Authority was no more than an isolated cluster among the uncountable suns known to humankind. But there wasn't one native, intelligent life form to be found in this entire part of space; a number of theories existed to explain why. The Authority had been chartered to exploit the incalculable wealth here. There were those who used words like "despoil" and "pillage" for what the Authority did. It maintained absolute control over its provinces and employees, and guarded its prerogatives jealously.

Leaning closer to Chewbacca, Han chuckled. "So the prospector says—get this, Chewie—the prospector says, 'Well how do you think my pack-beast got knock-kneed?' "

He had timed the delivery just right. Chewbacca had raised a two-liter mug of Ebla beer to his lips and a spasm of laughter caught him right in the middle of a long draught. He choked, snorted, and woofed mightily into his mug. White beer-spume exploded outward. Though they registered displeasure, patrons at nearby tables, inspecting the Wookiee and noting his size and the fierce, fanged visage, refrained from complaining. Han chortled, as he scratched a shoulder made itchy by the somatigenerative effects of the synthflesh.

Chewbacca uttered a guttural accusation. The pilot raised his eyebrows. "Of course I timed the punch line that way. Bollux told that joke to me while I was eating and it did the same thing to me." Chewbacca thought about the joke again and laughed abruptly, something halfway between a grunt and a bark.

Throughout his story and most of the long Bonadan morning Han had kept an eye on table 131. It was still vacant and the little red light over its robobartender indicated that it was still reserved. The closest overhead chrono showed that the time for Zlarb's rendezvous with his employer was long past.

The lounge was nearly filled, which tended to be true of this place at any hour of the day or night, what with the number of passengers and crew members passing through the port in addition to resident personnel. It was a light, airy, and open place constructed in levels of meandering terraces where plants

from hundreds of Authority worlds had been nur-
tured. Though every table had a clear view of the
constant traffic above, foliage tended to screen one
terrace from the next. The two partners had selected
a table from which they could observe table 131
through a lush curtain of D'ian orchid vine freckled
with sweet-smelling moss and still remain inconspicuous.

It had been their uncomplicated plan to observe
who came to meet Zlarb at the table, follow them out
and accost them, collecting their ten thousand by dint
of whatever threats or intimidation seemed appropri-
ate. But something was plainly wrong; no one had
come.

Han began feeling uneasy despite his joking; neither he nor Chewbacca was armed. Bonadan was a
highly industrialized, densely inhabited planet, one of
the Authority's foremost factory worlds. With masses
of humanity and other life forms packed together in
such number, the Security Police—"Espos," as they
were called in slangtalk—were at great pains to keep
lethal weapons out of the hands and other manipula-
tory appendages of the populace. Weapons detectors
and search-scan monitors were to be found almost
everywhere on the planet, including thoroughfares,
places of business, stores, and public transportation.
And, most particularly, surveillance was maintained
at each of Bonadan's ten sprawling spaceports, the
largest of which was Southeast II.

Carrying a firearm—either blaster or Wookiee bowcaster—would be grounds for immediate arrest, something the two could hardly afford. If their true identities
and past activities ever came to light, the Corporate
Sector Authority's only regret would be that it could
only execute them one time apiece. The one positive
aspect of this situation, the way Han saw it, was that
Zlarb's contact would in all probability be unarmed as
well.

Or, would have been. It was beginning to look like their wait had been for nothing.

Chewbacca punched a series of buttons on the robo-bartender and fed it some cash, very nearly their last. A panel slid back and a new round of drinks waited. The Wookiee took up a new mug enthusiastically, and for Han there was another half-bottle of a strong local wine. Chewbacca drank deeply and with obvious bliss, eyes closed, lowering the mug at last to wipe the white ring of suds out of his facial hair with the back of one paw. He closed his eyes again and smacked his lips loudly.

Han approached his bottle with less ardor. Not that he didn't like the wine; it was the intrusive nature of this overcivilized planet, as reflected in the design of the bottle, that he abhorred. He pressed hard on the cap's seal with his thumb and the cap popped off. Once off, it was almost impossible to re-affix. Then came the part Han really loathed; breach of the cap triggered the release of a small energy charge. Light-emitting diodes, manufactured into the bottle, began a garish show. Figures and lettering marched around the bottle extolling the virtues of its contents. The LEDs scintillated, giving what were intended to be winning statements about the wine's contents, bouquet, and the high standards of personal hygiene embraced by the bottler's employees and automata. Consumer information appeared, too, though in far smaller letters and less blinding hues.

Han, glaring at the bottle, refusing to touch it as long as it persisted in flaunting itself, thought *I should've had some of these back on Kamar. The Badlanders would probably've danced around them holding hands and singing hymns.*

After a minute or so the tiny charge was exhausted and the bottle reverted to an unaggressive container. Han's attention was attracted by a conversation going on by table Number 131, only a few meters away on the next terrace down. An assistant manager, a blue-furred, four-armed native of Pho Ph'eah, was engaged in a difference of opinion with an attractive young female of Han's own species.

The manager was waving all four arms in the air. "But the table is reserved, human! Can you not see the red courtesy light that so designates it?"

The human appeared to be several years younger than Han. She had straight black hair that fell just below the nape of her slender neck. Her skin was a rich brown, her eyes nearly black, indicating that she came from a world that received a good deal of solar radiation. She had a long, mobile face that showed, Han thought, a sense of humor. She wore an everyday working outfit—a blue one-piece bodysuit and low boots. She stood, hands gracefully on hips, and stared at the Pho Ph'eahian, unconvinced.

Then she contorted her face in a very close imitation of the manager's, waving her arms and shrugging her shoulders in precisely the way he had, though she was a couple of arms short. Han found himself laughing aloud. She heard him, caught his eye and gave him a conspiratorial smile. Then she went back to her dispute.

"But it's been reserved ever since I came in, hasn't it? And nobody's claimed it, have they? There're no other small tables and I'm tired of sitting at the bar; I want to wait for my friends right here. Or should we take our business elsewhere? It doesn't look like you're making much money off this table right now, does it?"

She had hit him in a vital spot. Lost revenue was something a good Authority employee simply never permitted. The blue-furred manager looked around worriedly to make sure the party or parties for whom the table was reserved wouldn't materialize out of thin air and object. With an eloquent four-shouldered gesture of resignation, he flicked off the red courtesy light.

The young woman took her place with a look of satisfaction.

"That's that," Han sighed to Chewbacca, who had noticed the incident, too. "No collections today; Zlarb's boss is as slippery as he was."

The Wookiee grumbled like a drumroll in a deep cave. He added a surly afterword as he rose to check on the *Millennium Falcon*.

"After you check the ship," Han called after him, "go hunt around the guild hiring halls and the portmaster's headquarters. I'll meet you later at the Landing Zone. See if anybody we know is in port; maybe somebody can tell us something. Chewie, if we don't come into some cash pretty soon, we're not even going to be able to get off Bonadan. I'm going to finish my wine, then make a few more stops to look for familiar faces."

The Wookiee, scratching his shaggy chest, acknowledged with a basso honk. As his copilot ambled off, Han took another sip of his wine and another look around, hoping that a last-minute arrival would give him a chance to pick up the ten thousand somebody owed him. But he saw no one who looked interested in table 131. Penury loomed before him and he felt the near-undeniable craving for money to which he was especially susceptible in times of financial distress.

He whiled away a few more minutes sipping at the wine and admiring the young woman who had pre-empted table 131. At length she happened to turn and catch his eye again. "Happy landings," she toasted, and he raised his glass in response to the old spacer's greeting. She eyed him speculatively. "Long time out?"

He made an indifferent face, not sure why she was interested. "No home port for me, just a ship. It's simpler."

She had drained her goblet. "How about a refill?"

Her lively, amused face appealed to him, and it didn't make much sense to carry on the conversation through intervening plantlife. He took his bottle and goblet and joined her at table 131.

"You and your friend were the only other ones keeping an eye on this table," she ventured as Han was refilling her goblet.

He stopped pouring. She reached out one forefinger and gently tilted the bottom of the bottle up, filling her goblet nearly to the brim.

"It was obvious, you know," she went on. "Every time someone approached this table, you and your sidekick looked as if you were going to jump through the foliage. I know; I'm very good at reading expressions."

Han was looking around for her backup men, support troops, deputies, accomplices, or whatever. Nobody else in the lounge that he could see was paying any particular attention. He had envisioned meeting a slaver's contact, someone hard and mean enough to stomach and prosper in one of the vilest enterprises there was. This attractive, breezy female had taken him completely off guard.

She sipped the wine. "Mmm, delicious. How are things on Lur, by the way?" She was now watching him vigilantly.

He kept his face blank. "Chilly. But the air's clearer than it is here." He batted the air with his hand. "Not as much smoke blowing around, know what I mean?" Sounding as casual as he could, he went on. "You have something for me by the way, don't you?"

She pursed her lips as if in deep concentration. "Since you bring it up we do have a little business. But the main lounge is a little public, wouldn't you say?"

"I didn't pick the place. Where would you suggest, sis, a dark alley? Down a mineshaft somewhere, maybe? Why meet here if not to take care of things?"

"Maybe I just wanted to look you over in the light." She glanced at an overhead chrono. "But you can take it for granted that you've been checked out and

approved. After I've left, wait ten minutes then follow." She slid him a folded durasheet with stylus markings on it. "Meet me at this private hangar. Bring proof
of delivery and you'll get your money." She raised
an eyebrow at him. "You *can* read, can't you?"

Han took the durasheet. "I'm better at feeling my
way. Why all the sneaking around?"

She gave him a sour look. "You mean why didn't I
just come up to you and dump a mound of cash on the
table and have you pass your receipt over? Work that
out for yourself."

She slid out of her seat and made her way out of
the lounge without a backward glance. Han enjoyed
the view in a dispassionate manner; she had a very nice
way of moving. His first impulse was to go find Chewbacca, and perhaps even take a chance on arming himself. But if he had to hunt the Wookiee among the
guild halls and portmaster's offices, it could take the
rest of the long Bonadan day. Han possessed what he
regarded as a certain flair for innovation, though, as
well as a confidence in his own ability to cope. None
of what the woman had said rang quite true, and her
allowing Chewbacca to leave before speaking to Han
definitely indicated that she was angling.

Still, minutes ago he had been worrying about
where his next meal was coming from, and now he
had what might be a chance to get the money he
felt was due him. That sort of thing always went a
long way toward quieting Han Solo's misgivings.

In any case, he had no intention of following her
instructions precisely. He would cheat enough to give
himself an advantage. After all, it was daylight and
the spaceport was buzzing with activity.

As soon as she was out of sight, Han rose to go. On
impulse he put a little more money into the robo-
bartender and got himself another half-bottle, taking
two more throwaway goblets from the dispenser. He
told himself *If she's on the level she might still be*

thirsty. I hope this makes up for grabbing her money.

Bonadan Spaceport Southeast II took in a larger square area than many cities, though little of it extended very high above or far beneath the planet's surface. There were shipbuilding and refitting yards, dock facilities for the barges and bulk freighters, an Espo command center, an Authority Merchant Marine academy, and the portmaster's headquarters. Added to that were passenger terminals, maintenance depots, ground transport installations, warehouses, and living and recreational arrangements for the thousands upon thousands of human and nonhuman types who either lived there or passed through Southeast II. Its immense expanse of fusion-formed soil supported fixed structures of permacite and shaped formex and more transient ones of quick-throw and lock-slab.

Because he had shipmaster's credentials, even though they were forged, Han didn't have to wait for the interport shuttleskimmer. Flagging one of the special courtesy cabs, he set off with the conviction that he could get across the huge port before the woman and whatever friends she might have.

He had the cab let him off a short distance from the hangar whose number she had given him. This part of the port was far less active; these hangars were rental structures, cheap, lock-slab constructions intended for private ships that might not be used for extended periods of time.

As he approached his destination, he passed one of the weapons detectors that covered Bonadan. It tracked him for a moment, like some exotic, overgrown flower following sunlight. Detecting no firearms on him it swung away without issuing an alarm. *Busybody,* grumped Han, hastening on his way.

Rather than enter the small rental hangar through the smaller portal set in the main doors, he located a rear door. It was unlocked and he did a prudent amount of listening and peeking-through before entering.

It was a windowless building containing some maintenance equipment and a compact, six-seater Wanderer. A number of tools lay around the Wanderer, suggesting that whoever had been working on her had gone out for some reason and left the rear door open.

Satisfying himself that the hangar was deserted, he found a place behind a pile of shipping crates, from which he could watch the main door without being seen. Hiking himself up onto an insulated shipping canister, he set down the goblets and half-bottle and waited. If the woman showed up with reinforcements, he'd be able to withdraw and follow them; if she came alone, Han figured, he'd soon be counting his money. Nevertheless, he began to wish Chewbacca was with him. He felt naked without his blaster, and the Wookiee's brawn would have been reassuring.

He was still thinking that when the lights went out.

Han jumped to his feet in a flash, pivoting slowly in absolute darkness without daring to breathe. He thought he heard sounds, a light skittering somewhere on or among the crates, but he couldn't get a fix on its direction. He had his hands and feet ready for defense but felt useless and quite vulnerable in the dark. He wished his sense of smell were as keen as Chewbacca's.

A weight hit his back and shoulders, driving him forward to hands and knees with a violence that knocked the breath from him. Then a rough, cold, damp surface was pressed up against his face. It felt like a hand within a heavy glove, but that was unimportant as he realized that the dampness was releasing fumes of some kind. He had caught his breath again when he had fallen and his reflexes kept him from getting more than a whiff, but that alone set his head spinning.

Fearing the anesthetic, Han tried to wrench his head away, but he succeeded only partially and the glove fumbled for him again. With a terrific effort he managed to continue holding his breath as he clamped down on the invisible hand and bit hard. His silent, invisible attacker wrenched madly and pulled the hand loose, breaking away.

Han lurched to his feet, head still swimming. He swung blindly, trying to land a blow or catch hold of his unseen opponent, but without effect. Rotating slowly, listening to his own heart pound, he was taken by surprise again as he was butted from behind.

Flying headlong, he struck the base of the shipping canister where he had been sitting. It was a double-walled container but luckily it was empty and light enough to yield somewhat. Still, he saw points of light circling before his eyes. He concluded woozily that his assailant must have taken the logical precautions of wearing snooper goggles and breathing filters as well, conferring an enormous advantage.

Something fell on Han's back and rolled onto the floor, then the attacker was on him again and it was all he could do to remember to hold his breath again. He struggled unsuccessfully to rise, protecting his head with one arm. As he did, his groping hand encountered something. It suddenly penetrated his dazed brain that what had landed on his back a moment before had been the half-bottle of wine, which he now held, jostled off the canister by the impact of Han's head. Unfortunately he was in no position to swing it, being held down by his assailant's weight on his back.

With desperate pressure of his thumb he broke the bottle's seal. The cap snapped off, and the bottle's combination LED light display and commercial advertisement began throwing out a garish light, dispelling the blackness.

The oppressive weight on his back shifted, then was gone. He could hear a scuffing of footsteps as his attacker retreated, confused or repelled by Han's unexpected trick. Han pushed himself back over, mouthing denunciations in four languages and trying to ignore the pain of his injuries and the effects of whatever it had been that he had inhaled.

He dragged himself up, using the canister for support. His attacker was nowhere in sight. Han held the half-bottle up but its glare didn't reach far into the gloom; the LEDs weren't, after all, meant for illumination.

He knew he had no time to waste looking for either his enemy or the controls to the lights. The minor charge that powered the bottle's LEDs would last only a little longer. He stumbled back to the hangar's rear door, trying to keep watch in every direction, without further incident.

Back in the glare of Bonadan's sun, he leaned against the hangar wall, closed his eyes and panted until his head cleared. The bottle was dimming. He tossed it aside and it bounced, rolling away rather than breaking. It was made of very tough glass.

What bothered him most was the thought that his attacker might have been the girl. He really thought she had been more kindly disposed toward him, but the facts seemed to add up. She would hardly be working alone, though, and that meant that both Han and Chewbacca might have been watched in the passenger lounge.

If Chewbacca had been followed from the lounge, he might really be in trouble.

Han sprinted off, looking desperately for a courtesy cab, hoping he would get to his ship before somebody tore her apart.

IV

THERE were, perversely, no courtesy cabs to be had in the private hangar area of the spaceport. Han used up long minutes at a dead run to locate one. The thought of his friend in desperate trouble, and that of possible damage to his beloved ship, kept him fuming and fidgeting the entire way. He was only marginally relieved when he saw the converted freighter resting, apparently unharmed, where he had left her.

Because they were short of funds, the partners had been compelled to leave their ship parked on an approach apron rather than in a rented docking bay as was their preference. Han took the ramp in two long bounds. Even before reaching the main hatch he had noticed, with a meticulous eye for every detail of his ship, a variety of tool marks and discolorations where power implements had been used. He covered the lock with his palm, ready to charge through the hatch the instant it rolled up, unmindful that he wasn't armed, all self-concern overriden by his anxiety over Chewbacca and fear that strangers were working who-knew-what atrocities on his source of freedom and livelihood, the *Millennium Falcon.*

But when the hatch was up he found himself, ready to spring into mortal combat, face-to-faceplate with Bollux. The 'droid's blank, glittering visage didn't convey much emotion, but Han could have sworn there was a note of relief in the vocoder drawl.

"Captain Solo! Are Max and I glad to see you, sir!"

Han brushed past him. "Where's Chewie? Is he all right? Is the ship all right? What happened? Who was here?"

"Aside from minor damage to the main hatch lock, all is in order. First Mate Chewbacca made a brief visual inspection earlier, and left. Then the surveillance systems alerted Max and me that someone was attempting to make a forced entry. Evidently the equipment they brought wasn't sufficient to compromise the ship's security arrangements."

That made sense to Han. The *Falcon* was no ordinary ship, and she had been modified to resist boarding or break-in efforts. Among other things, the relatively unsophisticated lock and other security gear had been replaced with the best Han could build, buy, or steal. Tools and equipment that could crack a stock freighter in minutes wouldn't even make the *Falcon* nervous.

Bollux continued his narration. "I warned them over the hatch comlink that I would alert port Espos if they didn't cease and desist and depart at once. They did, although in keeping with your standing orders I would have been very reluctant to involve any law-enforcement agency."

Han was back out at the ramp, checking the lock. Its palm plate showed nicks and scratches where a decoder had been fastened to it in a futile attempt to unlock it. The armored cover plate was scorched from a plasma torch or baffled blaster. The cover plate was barely touched and probably could have resisted entry for an additional fifteen to twenty minutes. It would have taken a light cannon to burn through in a hurry. But the damage to his ship left Han beside himself with outrage.

The labor 'droid went on, undaunted. "I went forward to the cockpit to observe them as they left."

"You stupid stack of factory rejects! You should've climbed down into the belly turret and erased 'em!"

Han was so angry he could scarcely see straight by now.

The 'droid's slow speech made him seem imperturbable. "That's one thing I could not do. I'm sorry, Captain; you know my built-in constraints against harming or attacking intelligent life forms."

Han, still brooding over the affront to his pride and joy, murmured, "Yeah. One of these days when I've got some time I'll have to see about those."

Alarmed at the thought of fundamental personality alterations as performed by Han Solo, Bollux quickly changed the subject. "Sir, I did get a view of the individuals who attempted to force entry. Both were human and wore blue standard coveralls. One was a man, but he wore a hat and I couldn't discern very much about him from the elevation of the cockpit. The other was a female with short black hair and—"

"I've met her," Han cut in, the color rising in his face. He was trying to calculate times and distances and determine whether it could have been her or her companion who had jumped him in the hangar. If, as he suspected, they had their own private transportation, it could easily have been. "Which way'd they go?"

"As a matter of fact, at Blue Max's suggestion I followed their departure through the macrobinoculars you keep in the cockpit. They parted and the man went off toward the passenger terminal, but the woman boarded a repulsorlift scooter, one of the green rental-agency models. In addition to her safety helmet, I noted, she was carrying a homing unit. Blue Max plugged into the ship's communication countermeasures package and resonated the homer; I've made a notation of the unit's setting. Then she flew away at a course of approximately fifty-three degrees west of planetary north, Captain."

Han was looking at Bollux in amazement. "You know, you two lads constantly wozzle me."

"You're very kind, sir." There was a brief squeal of electronic pulse-communication from deep within the 'droid's chest cavity. "Blue Max thanks you, too."

"A pleasure." Han considered his next move. The woman's course would take her out over some of the only open country in this part of Bonadan. He couldn't go after her in the *Falcon;* strict local airspace regulations prohibited taking spacecraft out of approach-departure corridors. The only remaining alternative was renting a repulsorlift scooter of his own and locating her that way. But that also meant going past who-knew-how-many more of the omnipresent weapons scanners and foregoing his blaster. Taking Chewbacca along would be a logical precaution, but waiting for the Wookiee to return decreased his chances of catching up with the woman. Han was still boiling about having been jumped in the hangar, madder still about the damage to the *Millennium Falcon,* minor though that was. In this sort of mood he had seldom been noted for his cool reasoning.

That left one more problem, communicating with Chewbacca. "Bollux, I want you to leave Max here, linked to the ship's surveillance system. If anybody else tries to tamper with the *Falcon,* he can do just what you did; if worse comes to worst, he can call in the Espos. Then I want you to go track down Chewie. He'll be either making the rounds of the guild hiring halls or portmaster's offices or waiting for me at a joint called the Landing Zone just outside the spaceport. I'll catch up with you both there as soon as I can or, if I'm gone more than a few hours, I'll meet you back here. Tell him everything that's happened."

The repulsorlift scooter was the fastest one the spaceport rental agency had, which was no particular mark of distinction. Han pushed the craft to its limits, its tiny engine sounding as if it had developed a lung

condition, scanning ahead with the macrobinoculars he
had brought from the ship.

He set a course to match the one Bollux had observed the woman to be taking. He had also brought
a homing unit, adjusted to the setting Blue Max had
resonated from hers.

The city was a dreary mosaic of factories, refineries,
offices, dormitories, worker housing, warehouses, and
shipping centers that stretched on and on. He
moved, as was required, through the lowest levels of
air traffic. Around him skimmers, gravsleds, and other
scooters passed and flowed according to the directions
of Traffic Control. Below, wheeled and tracked transportation and ground-effect vehicles moved along the
city's avenues and byways, and high overhead in the
hazy smog cover the lanes were monopolized by long-
distance mass transport craft, bulk haulers, and cargo
lifters. Espo patrol ships swam among the flow at all
levels like predatory fish.

Eventually he left the city behind, whereupon
Traffic Control notified him that guidance and naviga-
tion of his little vehicle had been returned to him. The
repulsorlift scooter was little more than a bucket-
chair with attached control board, a cheap, simple,
easily mastered vehicle common to any number of
worlds. He'd slung the visored safety helmet given
him by the rental agency from its storage clip at the
board's side; he wanted as wide a field of vision as he
could get. The fact that helmets were mandatory
didn't matter much to him.

Once out of the metropolitan restrictions, Han
poured on more speed than the scooter's engine was
supposed to be able to provide. Crouching behind the
little windscreen, he ignored the ominous noises coming
from the propulsion plant located under his seat.

Beneath him the surface of Bonadan came fully
into view for the first time—it was barren, parched,
eroded, and leached of its topsoil because plant life

had been destroyed by large-scale mining, pollution, and uncaring management. The surface was predominantly yellow, with angry strips of rust-red in its twisted gullies and cracked hillocks. The Corporate Sector Authority cared little about the long-range effects of its activities on the worlds it ruled. When Bonadan was depleted and unlivable, the Authority would simply move its operations to the next convenient world.

The landscape gave way gradually to steeper peaks and crags. These mountains must have had little mineral wealth and no industrial value, for they were relatively intact. The single incursion made here by the grasping technology of the Authority was an automated weather-control station, a titanic cylinder set lengthwise on its giant aiming apparatus. At present it was directed seaward, no doubt to dissipate a storm center the Corporate Sector Authority found inconvenient. To hell with Bonadan's natural weather patterns; ocean mining and drilling must go on, Bonadan's seas were dying.

The homing unit began registering. Han turned onto the course it indicated, hurdling the peak on which the weather station stood. He passed down over the lower hills beyond, scanning with the macrobinoculars, checking the homing unit from time to time.

A movement below caught his eye. Han brought the scooter to a hover while he focused on it more clearly. Another small air vehicle, something faster than a scooter, was dropping toward a flat table of land. Han could make out, already waiting on the ground, a tiny figure standing next to another scooter, a green rental job.

He cut in full thrust again. In a more leisurely moment he might have held off and surveyed the situation before going in, but he and his copilot had been cheated of ten thousand in cash and almost killed, which had made them vengeful ever since. Then somebody had pummeled Han to the ground and an attempt had been made to cut his ship open. Given conditions on Bonadan, the fact that no one below was likely to be carrying a firearm counted only lightly in his decision.

As he dove toward the ground, his rage built into something that was closer to an adrenalin seizure than to courage. He hit full emergency braking thrusters at the last instant, turning what should have been a prodigious crash into a startlingly abrupt precision touchdown, taking delight in the bone-shaking force of it.

Leaping from the scooter, Han was greeted by a dumbfounded stare from the woman and angry suspicion from the man who had landed just seconds before him. The man was a bit taller than Han, but very lean, with deep-set eyes and gaunt cheeks. He, too, wore standard worker's coveralls. The vehicle he had ridden, though, was far from commonplace. It was what was usually called a "swoop"—essentially an overpowered repulsor engine pod with handlebars. It was sitting on its landing skids, its engine making it throb gently.

The swoop-rider turned to the woman with an odd smile. "I thought you said Zlarb sent you alone." He then stared at Han. "You have a fatal sense of timing, friend." His hand dipped into the utility pouch on his belt. When it came up again it held something that filled the air with an insistent hum.

Han identified it as some sort of vibroblade, perhaps a butcher's tool or surgeon's instrument that the weapons scanners would register as an industrial implement. It had been home-altered to include a large blade, and its haft was fitted with a bulkier power pack. The blade, half again as long as Han's hand, was difficult to see, vibrating at an incredible rate. It would cut through flesh, bone, and most other materials with little or no resistance.

Han jumped backward as the vibroblade slit the air
where he had stood, its droning field sounding aroused
now. The woman's voice rang out firmly, "Just stop
right there!"

Both men saw that she had produced a small pistol,
but when she motioned with it the vibroblader
turned on her, blade held ready. His defiance put
doubt on her face, but she still pointed the weapon
directly at him.

"Quit fanning him with it and shoot!" Han yelled.
He saw her finger convulse at the trigger.

Nothing happened. She looked at the pistol in
amazement and tried to fire again with no more suc-
cess. The vibroblader turned to advance at Han again,
light-footed, making quick cuts and exploring Han's
defenses, which, in brief, were retreat and avoidance.
Against a regular blade Han might have tried to block
or parry; a simple laceration, even a deep one, could
be set right with the contents of any medipack and
would have been a price he would have accepted to
end the match. But a vibroblade would simply lop
off anything that got in its way; standard responses
would only get him carved to bits slowly.

Whoever he was, the vibroblader was good. Han
was suddenly and tardily sorry he had descended.
The man advanced at him more confidently now,
weaving his blade in the air, driving Han back step
for step, ready to leap forward in an instant if the
pilot turned to withdraw.

Han caught sight of his scooter out of the corner of
his eye. He side-stepped that way hastily, still facing
his opponent. The man circled that way just as
quickly, slashing where he thought Han would be, assuming he meant to escape.

But Han stopped and bent sideways at the last moment, snatching his safety helmet off its clip. Enraged
at having been tricked, the vibroblader hurried a
clumsy backhand stroke. Han swung the helmet by its

chinstrap with all his might but only caught the man with a badly aimed blow that bounced from his shoulder and glanced off the side of his head. The light material of the helmet wasn't enough to down him.

The vibroblader brought his weapon around and up in a move that would have opened Han vertically, but he had jumped back out of range. They shuffled on again, Han still retreating.

The fight had changed subtly. Han swung away with the helmet, aiming for the hand that held the weapon. Though he was still at a tremendous disadvantage, he just might connect, opening the vibroblader's guard. Then he might close with the man and immobilize his wrist, the only chance he needed.

But his opponent knew that as well as Han. His advance was still strong, but he was careful to avoid the flailing helmet. Then the vibroblader caught the safety helmet with a slash; a broad segment of the tough duraplas went flying free. Seeing that the helmet was too slow and clumsy, Han whirled what was left of it underhand and flung it upward at his opponent's face.

The man avoided it, ducking quickly to one side, but in that split second Han was inside his guard, his left hand around the wrist that held the weapon. Their free hands locked and they strained against one another. The man was far stronger than he looked; he forced his vibroblade nearer.

Han heard the dull burring of the knife's field by his left ear and, distracted by it, fell victim to a deft leg-trip. He fell to his back and the vibroblader fell with him, the two still locked together.

Han managed to roll over, gaining the top position, but his antagonist used the momentum to force another roll, regaining it and bringing Han up sharply against some unseen obstruction. The vibroblader rose a bit, using his weight, straining to bring the blade down. Its drone filled Han's ears as the duel

narrowed to a singleminded contest over the few
centimeters that separated the blade from Han's neck.

Suddenly the atmosphere of Bonadan seemed to be
filled with a tremendous roaring, a flood of sounds.
The vibroblader was ripped away so quickly that Han
was almost dragged with him. As it was, he was
hauled around, nearly wrenching his shoulder before
his grip was torn free of the other's hand and wrist.

Han sat up, confused. Looking in one direction he
saw the vibroblader lying some meters away, not doing a great deal of breathing. Turning his head slowly,
shaking it a little to clear it, Han saw the young
woman, off some distance in the other direction. She
was clumsily bringing the swoop around in a slow
turn.

She guided the vehicle with a jerky lack of skill.
Failing to coordinate braking thrust and lift, she
stalled it out completely. Giving it up, she dismounted
and finished the rest of the way back on foot. By
that time Han had risen and brushed much of the dust
off himself.

She studied him, left hand on hip.

"That wasn't a bad move, rocketsocks," he admitted.

"Don't you ever pay attention to anybody?" she
scolded. "I kept hollering 'look out, look out'; I was
going to toss a rock at him but you kept getting in the
way. I don't know what I would've done if he hadn't
been right behind the engine pod. If he'd been any
farther— Hey!"

Han had stepped forward, grabbed both her hands
and pulled her palms up roughly, inhaling them
deeply. He detected no scent of either the anesthetic
that had impregnated the gloves of his assailant at the
spaceport or any solvent that might have been used
to remove it. But her companion might have executed
the ambush in the hangar, or it was possible that the
stuff in the gloves might not have contacted her skin.

This didn't prove she was innocent; it only failed to prove she was guilty.

He let her go. She was watching him with arch interest. "Should I sniff you back or clap my hands on your nose or what? You're a really strange one, Zlarb."

That explained a few things anyway, if she meant it. "My name's not Zlarb. Zlarb's dead, and whoever he worked for owes me ten thousand."

She stared at him. "That tallies, provided you're telling the truth. But you were where Zlarb was supposed to be, doing more or less what he was supposed to be doing."

Han angled a thumb at the vibroblader's body. "Who was that?"

"Oh, him. That's who Zlarb was supposed to meet at the lounge. I was playing off both sides, Zlarb and his boss. Or, I thought I was."

Han began warming up to an interrogation session when she interrupted. "I'd love to chat this over at length but shouldn't we get out of here before *they* arrive?"

He looked up and saw what she meant. Bearing down on them was a flight of four more swoops. "Scooters are too slow. Come on." He snagged his macrobinoculars from his repulsorlift scooter and ran for the swoop belonging to the late vibroblader. Climbing on, he brought the engine pod back to life. The woman was bent over the vibroblader's body.

Working the handlebar accelerator, he tugged the swoop through a tight turn, helping with his foot. A quick surge of power took him to her side in a moment.

He braked hard. "Are you coming or staying?" he asked as he fit his knees into the control auxiliaries. She set her boot on a rear footpeg and swung up into the saddle behind him, showing him the vibroblade she had stopped to collect.

"Very good," he conceded. "Now belt in and hold on." He did the same, securing the safety belt tightly at his waist, and each donned a pair of the flying goggles that hung from clips at the swoop's side. He gave the accelerator a hard twist and they tore away into the air, the wind screaming at them over the swoop's low fairing. She clasped her arms around his middle and they both bent low to avoid the fairing's slipstream.

The oncoming swoops were approaching from the direction of the city, so Han turned deeper into open country. At the edge of the table of land he threw his craft into a sudden dive over the brink, straight down into a chasm beyond. The ground rushed at them.

He threw his weight against the handlebars and leaned hard against the steering auxiliaries. The swoop came up so sharply that he was nearly torn from the handlebars by centrifugal force and the woman's grip on him. The rearmost edge of the engine pod brushed the ground, making it skip and fishtail. Han just avoided a crash, slewed in midair and headed off down the sharply zigzagging chasm.

He calculated that, due to the steep, twisty nature of the gulches and canyons in the area, his pursuers couldn't simply stand off at high altitude and search for him, for he might escape through a side canyon or simply hide under an overhanging ledge and outwait them. If, on the other hand, they came in direct pursuit, they would have to hang on his tail through these obstacle course gullies and draws.

Han hadn't been on a swoop in years but had once been very good on them, a racer and a course rider. He was willing to match himself against the four who rode after him. The one thing that worried him was the chance that they might split their bet, one or two of them going high and the others clinging to his afterblast.

"What're you worried about anyway?" his passen-

ger yelled over the engine's howl and the quarrelsome
wind. "They won't have guns or that first man
would've had one, right?"

"That doesn't mean they can't jump us," he called
back over his shoulder, trying not to let it distract
him from negotiating the crazy turns and switchbacks
of the maze. He decided that she must have little experience with swoops. She made some remark he
didn't catch, sounding as if she understood, but he
was too busy conning the aircraft to answer.

Then he found out what she'd been worried about.
Coming out of an especially sharp turn he almost lost
control and had to touch his braking thrusters, swear-
ing at the necessity.

It saved both their lives. A sudden blast of force
erupted in the air to their right. Even the turbulence
at its very edge was nearly enough to send them into
the rock wall so close to their left. Under Han's desperate efforts the little swoop wobbled, then righted
and flew on.

Overhead and to the right banked one of the other
swoops; its pilot had brought it down in a steep dive
and snapped past, opening his accelerator at the
bottom of the dive in an effort to knock Han's vehicle
out of the air or tear its riders from their saddle with
the sheer force of an engine blast. Played for near-
misses and scares, this sort of thing had been a game
Han had known well in his youth; played for real, it
was an efficient form of murder.

He knew there would be at least one backup man;
they wouldn't leave more than half their number on
high cover. He came up on a forking of the way, took
a split second's bearing on the angle of the sun and
dodged into the canyon he had selected. The woman
was pounding him on the back, demanding to know
why he'd taken the more confining way.

There was a long overhang running along one side
of the canyon, but he clung to the other side, dividing

his time between the harrowingly fast decisions of the
ride and stolen, microsecond glances at the canyon
floor. He fought the urge to pull up and get clear of
the insane obstacle course; with its double burden,
his swoop would almost certainly be overtaken and
hemmed in and someone flying high cover was a good
bet to buffet him right out of the sky.

A flash of warning was all he got. The sun's slanting
rays showed him another shadow not far behind his
own on the canyon's floor. His instantaneous brake-
and-accelerate sequence was based more on intuition
than on computation of angles and speeds. But it
served its purpose; the other swoop overshot, its rider's aim thrown off by Han's maneuver. The other
rider pulled out of his dive, but by then Han had
pulled into a position to meet him as he brought his
swoop into an ascending curve. As he rose, the other
rider found himself gazing into the rear end of Han's
swoop's engine pod.

He couldn't avoid Han's afterblast. The other
swoop careened off the canyon floor, wobbled in the
air for a moment, then plowed into the ground. Han
didn't stop to see whether the rider survived the spill
or not; he poured on all the speed he safely could,
and considerably more besides. Climbing, diving, and
sideslipping, it was all he could do to keep from having a collision of his own.

It was a shock when, coming out of a frantic bank
that had their swoop's underside within centimeters
of a vertical canyon wall, Han and his passenger
broke into the open, leaving the hills behind. Unexpectedly, the other three pursuers, who had lost
track of Han in the maze, came flying at an almost
leisurely pace across his course.

He had a moment's view of their astounded faces,
a human and two humanoids whose gold-sheened
skins gleamed in the hazy sunlight of the long Bona-

dan afternoon. They swung their swoops around to re-
sume the chase as Han accelerated.

Even as he did, he knew a straight run would be
futile. With the woman aboard he was bound to be
overtaken before he could reach the safety of the
patrolled city traffic patterns. What he needed was
something to break off the pursuit.

Something off to his left attracted his attention. The
huge cylinder of the automated weather-control station was just beginning a slow swing on its aiming
apparatus, realigning for a new assignment. Han
yanked at the handlebars and cut a new course for it.

His passenger screamed. "What are you doing?
They'll catch us!"

He couldn't take time to tell her they would be
overtaken anyway. Closing fast on the station's supporting framework, he had to cut speed. Quick looks
told him that his swoop was being bracketed above
and to either side by the remaining pursuers. He cut
speed even more as the support framework loomed
directly before him.

For the moment his pursuers held back, not sure
why he was riding straight at this huge obstruction.
They had no desire to be lured into a fatal accident.

At the last second he shed almost all his speed and
threaded in through the girderwork support. It wasn't
a particularly hard maneuver; the thick girders were
widely spaced, and his speed was, by then, com-
paratively low. The pursuers, closely grouped behind
him, chose to follow rather than detour around the
support tower. They were determined not to lose him
as he broke out the other side. That wasn't, however,
his plan.

He pulled at the handlebars and went into a
vertical climb, straight up the central well of the support tower, hoping that this station followed standard
design.

It did; he shot between two catwalks and directly

out into the cavernous emission cylinder, a gridwork
with open squares some meter and a half or so on a
side. The emission cylinder was 150 meters long, less
than a third of that in diameter. He swung down toward one end of the slowly rotating cylinder, orient-
ing himself and figuring out just which way the station
was pivoting.

He turned back to see the three pursuers soar into
the cylinder in determined chase. They were moving
a good deal slower than Han; they had never played
this game before.

"Stay gripped," he shouted over his shoulder and
swung back toward the others. The cylinder was more
than spacious enough for them to scatter and avoid
him, thinking he was trying to ram. Then they
dropped in on his tail again, following him down toward the far end of the cylinder where, they were
sure, they could trap and halt him.

Until he speeded up again. The engine pod blared
its power. The far end of the emission cylinder was
still swinging and Han had to compensate carefully for
its movement. He crouched forward, sighting carefully through the fairing, lining up the swoop precisely.
The openings in the gridwork were frighteningly small.

The woman saw what he was about to do and bur-
rowed her head into his back. The opening he had
selected expanded before him. There was a terrible
moment of doubt, far too late to change his mind.

The gridwork passed him like a shadow. And he
was in the open, pointed more or less toward the city,
the swoop's engine howling. He took a quick look behind. Pieces of wreckage were raining slowly to the
ground and some lengths of gridwork stuck out jag-
gedly; one of his pursuers had tried to emulate him
and failed.

The woman's face was pallid.

"Are you all right?" he asked.

"Just fly this thing, you psychopath!" she shouted back.

He faced forward again with an arrogant smirk. "Deft hands and a pure heart triumph again! You were never in any—" He gulped as he saw that the top edge of the fairing had been neatly sheared away. He'd been spared by no more than millimeters.

"—danger," Han Solo finished in a much more subdued voice.

V

CHEWBACCA, still some distance from the *Millennium Falcon,* smelled a strange odor and knew something was wrong. Black nostrils flaring in a futile effort to identify the aroma, he approached the starship as quietly as he could. Despite his great size and weight, the Wookiee, a veteran hunter, moved with total stealth.

After leaving the lounge, Chewbacca had made only a cursory check of the *Falcon,* eyeballing her to make sure no one on any of the grounds crews had attempted to move the freighter or block her in. Then he had begun a round of inquiries at the portmaster's headquarters and guild hiring halls. But the *Falcon's* first mate had turned up nothing of use.

His errand had caused him to miss both the abortive attempt to break into the ship and Han's subsequent appearance and departure. But now he had discovered still another threat to the starship. Silently easing up to the foot of the ramp, he saw an unfamiliar form hunched over and working busily at the freighter's main hatch lock. Next to the figure was an open tool bag containing a fusioncutter, some probes, a drill, and other instruments of illegal entry. The intruder's ears were covered with some sort of headphones.

Chewbacca ascended the ramp like a wraith, reached out, seized a broad handful of the nape of the intruder's neck, and lifted. The headphones shook

loose and from the creature's neck dangled the thing
to which they were attached, apparently a listening
device for the opening of locks.

"Eee-ee!" The figure writhed and wriggled with
such sinuosity that the Wookiee lost his hold. But as
the would-be burglar sought to dodge past him,
Chewbacca's long arms scooped out to either side,
blocking the way. Trapped, the intruder shrank back
against the *Falcon's* main hatch, panting and trembling.

The being was small, perhaps a head shorter than
Han Solo when standing erect rather than cowering.
He had the sleek, glossy pelt of an aquatic mammal,
colored a deep gleaming black. He was a biped with
short, strong-looking fingers and toes; between those
fingers and toes were webs of pinkish-gray skin.
He had a thick, tapering tail and pointed ears that
stood close to his skull, moving independently, aiming this way and that, first at the Wookiee, then away.
His long, moist snout snuffled and quivered nervously. From this whiskered snout protruded a set of
long buckteeth. It was plain from his squinting eyes
that his vision wasn't very acute.

The being seemed to gain a good deal of information by his ears; Chewbacca assumed it was only because he had been wearing the headphones that he'd
failed to notice the Wookiee's approach.

The intruder collected himself and drew himself
up to his full height (which wasn't very imposing
against Chewbacca's), nose quivering and tail vibrating in righteous indignation. Unfortunately his voice,
when it came, was something of a quavering squeak
with a slight lisp, reducing the effect. Still, it held
conviction.

"What's the idea of assaulting me, you big over-
stuffed oaf of a Wookiee? How *dare* you? I'll have
you know I'm a licensed collections agent. This vessel
appears on the *Red List!"* He snagged a card out of

his open bag and presented it with the formal flourish of a webbed hand.

It was a document of identification and authorization for one Spray, of the planet Tynna, to act in the interests and on the behalf of Interstellar Collections Limited, pursuant to the collection of debts, garnishing and repossession proceedings and any and all activities connected thereunto. On it was a flat two-dee depicting the little collections agent.

Chewbacca, satisfied that the document was real, looked up with a snarl of displeasure directed at all skip-tracers in general and at Spray in particular. Like Han, he sincerely detested them.

Jumping out on a debt seldom meant trouble with law enforcement agencies; it was such a common practice among members of the fringe society of independent spacers that every lawman in the galaxy could have spent every waking moment looking for, apprehending, and prosecuting them to the exclusion of all other activity. Thus the Espos, Imperial forces, and other legal authorities tended to ignore the problem, leaving the collection of debts and/or repossession of spacecraft to agency skip-tracers like Spray who roamed the galaxy with the voluminous and infamous *Red List*.

Spray appeared not to notice the Wookiee's snarl. Having identified himself, he reverted to being a company man. The Tynnan dug out, from somewhere, an incredibly thick little notebook, squinting into it, his moist nose nearly touching the page.

He mumbled to himself as he read. "Ah, here, yes," he said finally. "Would you by any chance be Captain, um, Solo?"

Chewbacca barked an irritated negative and jerked a thumb back at the spaceport, indicating Han's present location as well as he could. Then he moved Spray rudely out of his way and bent to see what had been done to the lock. When he noticed the same damage

Han had seen earlier he let out a horrible howl and turned back on the skip-tracer with mayhem in mind.

But the Tynnan, back on familiar territory, was indignant rather than intimidated. He snuffled. "I most certainly am *not* responsible for that damage! Do you mistake me for a bungler and a thug? A brainless primitive unconversant with modern technology? I am a trained collections agent, my dear Wookiee, equipped with the latest tools of my profession; I avoid doing any unnecessary damage to repossessed property. I have no idea who was tampering with the hatch lock before me, but you may depend upon it that it wasn't *me!* I simply deactivated the surveillance system and was about to neutralize the lock —*without* damaging it, if I may say so—when you so violently accosted me. Now that you're here, however, the need no longer exists."

Spray was burrowing his bucktoothed proboscis into his notebook again and lisping mumbles to himself, insinuating himself between the Wookiee and the *Falcon*'s main hatch. Chewbacca found himself somewhat off stride; his wrath and threats were sometimes greeted by fear, sometimes by hostility, and occasionally with combat, but never had the towering first mate met anyone quite so preoccupied that he actually paid him no attention.

"Ah, here we are," Spray went on, having riffled back to the correct page. "Your captain has failed to settle on an outstanding debt of some two thousand five hundred Credits Standard owed to Vinda and D'rag, Starshipwrights and Aerospace Engineers Incorporated, of Oslumpex V. Your Captain Solo has ignored seven—no, eight dunning notices."

He glared myopically at the Wookiee. "*Eight*, sir. Vinda and D'rag have therefore presumed default on your captain's part and referred the matter to my employers. Now, if you'll be good enough to open the hatch, I can continue the repossession process. Of course, you're free to remove all personal effects and non—"

Chewbacca had been making deep, reverberating noises in his throat up to now, which someone more familiar with him would have taken as a danger signal. His annoyance burst forth in a roar that drove Spray back a step with its sheer physical impact, ruffling the little skip-tracer's nose fur and bending back his whiskers.

But he stood waiting patiently, eyes squeezed shut against the vocal gale, as Chewbacca railed horrible Wookiee oaths at him. The Tynnan flinched every now and then as the crescendo rose, his ears swinging back protectively, but he held his ground resolutely. The *Falcon*'s first mate periodically punctuated his ranting by slamming his enormous fist against the ship's hull, evoking deep percussives from her armor.

But when he finally ran down, Spray began again in the mildest of tones. "Now then, as I was saying: I have a document here entitling me to take possession of—"

Chewbacca snatched up the papers proffered by Spray. It was a thick legal instrument of several pages; the Wookiee crushed it into a tightly compressed wad in his powerful hands and stuck it into his fanged mouth. Sneering hideously at the skip-tracer, he chomped on the document a few times, shredding it handily, then swallowed it.

But it did little to alleviate his frustration over how to deal with Spray. This was the first time in memory that Chewbacca had ever had such difficulty with a creature whom he outweighed three to one. He was beginning to feel embarrassed; the scene had already attracted the attention of several local idlers and a number of passing automata. The idea of simply demolishing the Tynnan was now out of the question.

"That will do you precisely no good whatsoever, my dear Wookiee," Spray hastened to assure him. "I have many duplicates. Now, unless your captain is prepared to make immediate and total defrayal of the entire sum of his debt, I'm afraid I *must* demand that you open that hatch, or permit me to do so."

Chewbacca surrendered at last, growling and motioning Spray to follow him back down the ramp. He would take the skip-tracer to talk to his partner; he could see no alternative short of losing the ship or committing premeditated murder in a public place.

But Spray was shaking his head briskly, his whiskers quivering. "I'm afraid it just won't do, my good fellow. It's too late to begin negotiating; immediate payment or immediate repossession are your only choices."

In the course of a long life Chewbacca had learned that there come times when the most bellicose roar is insufficient. He clamped one vast paw on either of Spray's shoulders and effortlessly hoisted the skip-tracer up close, until their gazes were level. Suspended furry muzzle to bucktoothed muzzle with Chewbacca, his webbed feet dangling somewhere above the Wookiee's knees, the Tynnan watched as the *Millennium Falcon*'s first mate wordlessly peeled his lips back from ferocious rows of teeth.

"Then again," the collections agent resumed hastily, "perhaps we *could* work out some sort of agreement and spare my employers the expense and inconvenience of public auction. Point well taken, sir. Where might I find your captain?"

Chewbacca carefully set Spray back down on his feet and, gesturing to the lock surveillance system, growled harshly. Taking his meaning clearly, Spray dug some tools from his bag and quickly reactivated the device.

Blue Max's chirp instantly sounded over the intercom. "Who's there? Why was this instrument deactivated? Reply at once or I'll notify port security!"

Chewbacca barked once at the comlink. "Oh, First

Mate Chewbacca, sir," Max replied happily. "I thought the ship was being burglarized again. There was already one attempt earlier. Captain Solo's gone off to investigate. He dispatched Bollux to the Landing Zone with word, and said he'd meet you there. Are you coming aboard, sir?"

The Wookiee barked irritably as he marched Spray down the ramp. The Tynnan had to trot to match Chewbacca's long strides.

Blue Max called after them. "But what are my instructions?"

As the Wookiee dragged him off, the skip-tracer shrilly called back, "In the name of Interstellar Collections Limited, make sure no harm comes to that vessel!"

"What's your name, anyway?" the woman asked as they passed through the entrance to the Landing Zone. It was a well-known spot among spacers, prominent on the avenue of bars, rub-shops, gambling dens, and pawnbrokers' establishments outside the spaceport's main crew gate. "Mine's Fiolla," she encouraged.

Han hadn't had much chance to talk to her on the ride back, at the end of which they had abandoned the swoop and the vibroblade several blocks away, in the middle of the teeming Alien Quarter. It was a good bet that the swoop already had a new coat of paint or was dismantled.

But he saw no reason to cudgel his brain for a cover; the slavers already knew his name, and anyone else who wanted to badly enough could find out.

"Han Solo," he said. She gave no sign of recognizing it.

Bollux, having failed to find Chewbacca in the spaceport's wide confines, had had no more luck at the Landing Zone. But by soliciting the bartender's permission with particular fervor, he had been allowed to wait by the entrance.

Now he approached Han who, sighting the 'droid, sighed. "I don't feel like talking standing up. Come and have a seat, Bollux."

The Landing Zone and all its furnishings were built from pieces and fittings from the spaceport salvage yards. Han led the way to a small table made from an obsolete charts-computer from an old survey ship.

When Bollux and Fiolla had taken seats he turned to her. "Bollux, general labor 'droid, at your service."

Han interrupted Fiolla's courteous reply. "Never mind that," he snapped. "Bollux, where's Chewie?"

"I was unable to locate him, Captain. I came here assuming this to be the place where you'd eventually contact him."

The waiter came by, a many-tentacled Sljee with a broad tray firmly fastened to the top of its low, slab-shaped body. There was a hole in the middle of the tray and through it the Sljee's olfactory antennae waved like some strange centerpiece.

"What're you folks having?" it asked them hurriedly, the second afternoon rush just having begun. Then it noticed Bollux. "Sorry, but it's against house policy to allow 'droids at the tables. You two gentlemen will have to leave him outside."

"*Who's* a gentleman?" Fiolla demanded sharply.

"Beg pardon," apologized the Sljee. "I've only been working here since this morning. It's my first time away from home and I've never dealt with aliens before. Non-Sljee, I mean. The smells are so confusing. Frightfully sorry."

"The 'droid stays," Han stated flatly. "Now go bring us two Flameouts, or I'll tell the manager you insulted this lady. I'm a very close friend of his."

"At once, sir. Coming right up." The Sljee pirouetted on its many short podia and sailed off in the direction of the service bar.

"So we know I'm not Zlarb," Han resumed to
Fiolla. "Who are you not?"

She chuckled. "I'm not a slaver, but you know my
real name, or at least part of it. I'm Hart-and-Parn
Gorra-Fiolla of Lorrd, Assistant Auditor-General,
Corporate Sector Authority."

An Authority exec, Han groaned to himself. *Why
don't I just go down to the Espo prison, pick a comfortable cell, and get it over with?* Instead he pursued
the conversation. "Slavers must have interesting au-
dits, fascinating expense vouchers."

"Doubtless, but I've never read one. I'm an
auditor-at-large, sort of a roving assignment conducting random checks of Authority operations. I was
working here with my assistant when I found out that
there's a slavery ring operating inside the Authority.
Some top execs are implicated, and a number of Espo
officials. I think it might go as high as the territorial
manager for this entire part of the Authority, Odumin,
and that's a shock in itself. Although I've never met
him, I've heard that Odumin's always shunned the
limelight, but he's always been a decent administrator,
a regular humanitarian as managers go. Anyway, I'm
conducting my own investigation. When I've developed all the information, I'm going to dump it right
in the lap of the Board of Directors."

She smiled brightly. "Then I'm going to nail myself
the juiciest promotion and raise you ever saw. You're
looking at Fiolla of Lorrd, heroine of the spaceways.
Now how about you?"

He spread his hands. "I fly for hire. I rendezvoused
with Zlarb without knowing he wanted me to move
slaves. We disagreed and he got shot. And I don't
care who's doing what to whom; I've got ten thousand in cash coming and I want it. Zlarb had a tape
message to meet someone here for payment so I kept
his appointment. How did you end up there in the
lounge?"

"It was part of the information I came across. Did Zlarb tell you anything else?"

"Zlarb made the Final Jump shortly after being burned with a disruptor, but he had a record of ship registrations and leasing permits. Almost all of them were funneled through an agency on Ammuud."

She was listening distractedly, but he went on. "Do you mind telling me how come I'm in your confidence all of a sudden? Not that it doesn't stir me deeply, of course."

"Simple; this thing's even bigger than I'd thought. I need some additional help and I can't go to the Espos. You seem to know what you're doing in an unsubtle sort of way. And you definitely aren't a member of the slavery ring unless murder is a standard business pay-down."

"You'd be surprised. But don't get any ideas; I'm not the helpful type. How'd you end up out there today, by the way?"

"My assistant, Magg, got his hands on a message that the management was holding for Zlarb back there at the lounge. When I decided you weren't going to tell me much I sent you off to chase yourself and—"

Han leaned forward with a certain look on his face that caused Bollux to fear for Fiolla's safety. "And Magg followed me to put my lights out, right?"

She looked honestly shocked. "Are you saying someone attacked you?"

"Somebody did everything except zeroize my rotors."

She drew a deep breath. "I gave you the number of an Authority pool hangar. The ship there was the one Magg and I arrived in. I knew it was on down time, waiting for parts, and there'd be no one around. But listen—Magg trailed your hairy friend when he left the lounge and that's how we found out which ship was yours. When we couldn't get aboard for a search, I went off to keep Zlarb's appointment myself because the instructions said one person and one scooter. I sent Magg to see what he could find out about you."

Han was so busy trying to unravel what she had said that he forgot to be angry at her mention of the attempted break-in. He was impressed with her resourcefulness, antagonized a bit by her self-assurance, and surprised by her naïveté.

The Sljee waiter had returned. Two tentacles whisked two tall glasses off its back-tray while two more placed absorbmats before Han and Fiolla. "There we are," the Sljee said cheerfully. "Will that be pay as you go, or shall I put it on a tab?" it asked hopefully. It had already been stiffed twice that day by unscrupulous customers who had taken advantage of its difficulty in differentiating among individual non-Sljee.

"Run the tab," said Han immediately. The Sljee retreated in disappointment, trying its best to memorize Han's odor without much confidence.

The Flameouts were perfect, burning their tongues and freezing their throats, making them gasp a bit. "Don't you think it was stupid to ride out there alone?" Han asked.

"I had a gun," she argued. "A special, one that doesn't register on scanners. Lots of execs carry them. How did I know the worthless thing would let me down?"

"Where's your assistant now?"

"After Magg checks on you he'll go to our hotel and get ready to leave. It occurred to me that we might have to get off-planet in short order."

"Very possible," allowed Han. A sudden thought struck him and he became hostile again. "I owe Magg for damaging my ship, don't I?"

"I ordered him to try to break in, to see if there was any information onboard; I thought you might just be playing very, very dumb. If you want to get even, you can take me on another swoop ride some-

time. By the way, what kind of security system is that
you've got? Magg was sure he could open up a
freighter without breaking stride, but that lock of
yours stopped him cold. He said he'd need a tool
shop to get in."

"I like my privacy," Han explained simply, avoiding the mention of smuggling.

"Magg said it was like trying to crack the Imperial
Currency Reserve."

"Sounds like an experienced guy."

"Oh, very versatile, yes. I handpicked him because
he had, ah, a range of abilities. I think you two will
find one another quite—"

At that moment Chewbacca arrived with Spray.
The Wookiee forcefully sat the little Tynnan down
with the pressure of a giant paw and took a seat himself, filling it to overflowing.

"I met Fiolla here and almost got killed," Han told
his friend pleasantly. "How was *your* afternoon?"

Chewbacca studied the woman with his large, lucid
blue eyes and she returned the scrutiny. Then the
Wookiee motioned to Spray and, in his growling,
barking language, explained to Han what had happened as the skip-tracer squinted from one to the
other.

"I hate skip-tracers," announced Han Solo at length.

"In that case I think I'll just be toddling along . . ."
Spray said, starting to rise. Chewbacca clapped a paw
on him and pushed him back down.

Han's head was spinning with this new develop-
ment, and he wished he could process information as
quickly as Blue Max. Theoretically, Spray could enlist
the aid of the Espos in taking possession of the
Falcon. Once again Han wondered when his string of
rotten luck would break.

Just then the Sljee waiter showed up again, having
noticed Chewbacca's and Spray's presence. It en-

deavored to speak in its most hospitable tones, still
aware of its previous gaff.

"Yes, *sir*," purred the Sljee to the Wookiee, "and
what can I bring you and your strapping young hatch-
ling here?"

Chewbacca snarled at the Sljee. Spray, already visibly disturbed, exploded. "We're not even the same
species!"

"What've I told you about that?" Han asked the
Sljee menacingly.

"A thousand pardons," wailed the Sljee, rotating
back and forth through nervous quarter-turns and in-
tertwining its tentacles imploringly.

"What in the world is going on?" Fiolla wanted to
know, not having understood anything Chewbacca
had said.

Spray held his paws up, webbed fingers spread,
until the others were quiet, including the Sljee. "First
of all, we have no need of any refreshments, thank
you," the Tynnan told the waiter. The Sljee retreated
gratefully.

"Now," Spray continued, "the central issue, Captain Solo—please stop *shush*ing me, sir; I will be
heard! At issue are two thousand five hundred Credits
Standard owed Vinda and D'rag, Starshipwrights.
Unless you're prepared to make payment, I am em-
powered to attach and take possession of your ship,
which, by the way, appears to have had her marking
altered in illegal fashion."

Han narrowed his eyes and glared at Spray. "I am
thinking right now," he said, "of how a certain chisel-
beaked runt is going to get his just desserts."

"It's a bit public for threats of aggravated assault,
isn't it, Solo?" Fiolla asked.

"You keep out of this! For all I know, you two work
together."

"Bullying will do you no good, Captain," Spray
plowed on insistently in his squeaky voice. "Either

remittance arrangements must be made this very
moment or I shall be forced to go to the portmaster
and the Security Police."

Han had his mouth open, uncertain whether he
would try to lie or simply instruct Chewbacca to ren-
der the skip-tracer unconscious. He heard Fiolla say:
"*I'll* pay for him."

Han's mouth stayed open as he turned on her.
"Better close it," Fiolla cautioned, "before your
tongue gets sunburned. Look, this problem of mine is
a lot more complicated than I'd thought. It will take
more investigation before I'm ready to go to the Board
of Directors. I need a way to get around fast, and I'm
not particularly anxious to go by public transportation.
And the last thing I want is to take an Authority pool
ship. Solo, you ought to be eager to leave, too, before
the Espos start asking about missing rental scooters
and several swoop riders smeared out on the landscape. If you'll charter out to me, I'll cover your debt.
Besides, you want your ten thousand, don't you? Your
best chance of finding it is to stick with me."

She turned to Spray. "How about it?"

The Tynnan nervously scratched up tufts of fur on
his skull, blinking and wriggling his nose back and
forth in consternation. "Cash?" he asked at last.

"An Authority Cash Voucher," Fiolla replied. "Half
now, half when we're done. They're as good as money
in a vault."

"Interstellar Collections Limited does prefer re-
payment to repo procedures," the skip-tracer admitted. "But I'm afraid I couldn't let you out of my
sight until restitution is made."

"Just a second," Han snapped at Fiolla. "I'm not
carting that little bloodsucker along anywhere."

Spray remained unexpectedly firm. "Captain Solo,
her proposal is absolutely the only alternative to having your ship attached."

"There's always the famous Disappearing Skip-Tracer Trick," suggested Han darkly.

"Be civilized," Fiolla chided. "This won't take long, Solo. And if you don't help me, maybe I'll have to drag your name into my report. But if you take me to check out this shipping agent on Ammuud, the one you mentioned, I'll forget about you completely."

Han hoped it would be mutual. He poured down half of what remained of his Flameout. It felt corrosive but didn't help much otherwise. He looked to his first mate, who was looking back, no help at all, willing to go with whatever decision Han made.

He put his chin on his fist. "Chewie, you take Bollux and paddlefoot, here, back to the ship. I'll go with our new employer and pick up her assistant. Get liftoff clearance and punch up a jump to Ammuud."

Fiolla scribbled quickly on a pad of forms and pressed her thumbprint against the authorization square. She presented the voucher to Spray, whereupon Han realized that she was carrying an open expense account and that her position with the Authority must be an important one indeed.

The Wookiee had risen and moved near Spray as a general precaution, with Bollux close behind. But the Tynnan only made a polite parting bow to Fiolla. "Thank you for remaining reasonable about this entire incident," he said.

He started for the door. Chewbacca growled a farewell to Han, then to Fiolla. She returned it, not getting the vocal sounds right but contorting her face around into a very close approximation of the Wookiee's, even to getting both corners of her upper lip up high and baring her lower teeth along with the uppers in true Wookiee fashion. Chewbacca was startled, but yipped laughter. Then he went quickly, Bollux at his side, to catch up with the departing Spray.

"You're a pretty good mimic," Han commented,

remembering her imitation of the four-armed manager in the terminal lounge.

"I told you, I'm from Lorrd," she reminded him, and he understood. The Lorrdians had, for many generations, been a subject race during the Kanz Disorders. Their masters had forbidden them to speak, sing, or otherwise communicate as they worked at their slave labors. The Lorrdians had evolved a complicated language of extremely subtle hand and facial movements and body signals and become masters of kinetic communication. Although it had been generations since their servitude had been ended by the Jedi Knights and the forces of the Old Republic, the Lorrdians remained among the galaxy's very best mimes and mimics.

"So that's how you knew Chewie and I were watching table 131 today?"

"I read you like a pair of message tapes; you tipped it every time someone went near the table."

And, thought Han, Fiolla's Lorrdian background gave her an added interest in ending the slavery ring. Still, it was unusual to find a Lorrdian working this far from home, and especially for the Corporate Sector Authority.

About to down the last of his Flameout, Han pointed to the open voucher pad. "There are plenty of times when you can get more with a blaster than with one of those, but if I had one I'd buy myself a nice little planet and retire."

"Which is why you'll never have one," she assured him, rising and following him from the table. "This slavery business is going to be my big break; nothing's keeping me out of a Board chair."

The Sljee waiter returned, its olfactory stalks tilting and waving when it took cognizance of the empty table. Then it noticed Han and Fiolla and approached them tentatively, the check extended before it on a metal salver.

"Ah, I believe this is your check, humans," ventured the Sljee.

"Us?" Han, who was broke, cried indignantly. "We just arrived, and for your information we've been waiting to be seated for quite a while now. And you're trying to stick us with somebody else's check when we haven't even had a drink yet? Where's the manager?"

The Sljee was spinning around and back, tangling its tentacles in total consternation. Its sensory equipment was really quite excellent at fine distinctions and subtle perceptions concerning other Sljee, but it found humanoid species dreadfully anonymous.

"Are you certain?" the Sljee moaned abjectly. "I'm sorry; I, I suppose I had you confused with two others." It studied the vacant table, wringing its tentacles in distress. "You didn't happen to see them leave, did you? If I'm stiffed again it will cost me my job."

Unable to endure any more, Fiolla drew a generous handful of cash from her thigh pouch and tossed it on the salver. "Solo, you're impossible."

The Sljee withdrew, showering her with its gratitude. Fiolla headed for the door.

"It's every life form for himself," opined Han Solo.

VI

FIOLLA'S hotel was, predictably, the finest lodging place at the spaceport, the Imperial. Han tried his best not to look uncouth and out of place as he followed her through a lobby of soaring gem-set columns, vaulted ceilings, resilient plush carpeting, delicate glow-orb lighting, expensive furnishings, and lush shrubbery.

Fiolla, on the other hand, was a picture of cool, nonchalant poise, aristocratic even in coveralls. She led the way to the lift shaft and punched for the seventieth level.

Her suite was luxurious without being overdone. Han suspected that, though Fiolla could have afforded something far showier, she would have deemed it vulgar.

But the second she palmed her door open, he knew something was wrong. Things were in disorder. Conform-lounge furniture had been pushed and shoved out of place, suspension cushions and floater pads ripped or overturned. Storage panels were hanging open and the data plaques and tapes with which Fiolla worked were strewn all over the floor.

As Han pulled Fiolla out of the doorway, he suddenly remembered that he was unarmed. "Do you have another gun?" he whispered to her. She shook her head, her eyes very wide. "Then give me the special; it's better than nothing."

She passed the inoperative weapon to him. He

listened closely but heard no sound to indicate that
whoever had ransacked her room was still there. He
moved cautiously into the suite, listening at each
doorway before he went through. He found signs of
search everywhere on his wary sweep, but satisfied
himself that no one remained in the rooms.

He engaged her door's security mode at FULL ISO-
LATION. "Where's Magg's room?"

She pointed. "There's a connecting door behind
that hanging; we usually take adjoining quarters. An
audit can demand very long hours."

Sliding Magg's door open slowly, ear cocked for any
warning, he heard none. Magg's suite was in the same
state as Fiolla's.

"You sent him back here to pack?" Han asked.
Fiolla nodded, gazing around the ransacked place in
some shock. "Well, somebody forwarded him for you.
Grab whatever you can put in your pockets; we're
getting out of here right now."

"But what about Magg? We have to report this outrage to the Espos." Her voice trailed away as she
returned to her own suite. He began feeding instructions into the programming panel for the servant-
drones that took care of domestic chores, then went
back to Fiolla's suite.

"We don't go to any Espos," he called to her.
"They may be part of it, isn't that what you told me?
Then don't go cutting the charter short."

He began inserting orders into the programming
panel for her rooms, too. Fiolla returned, her various
coverall pockets and pouches bulging and a slim day-
tote slung over one shoulder. "I don't like it, but
you're correct about the Espos," she admitted. "What
are you doing?"

He turned from the panel. "Well, what do you
know, a female who can travel light. What I did was
issue instructions for your stuff and Magg's to be put
into storage. You can come back for it later"—*I hope,*

he thought to himself. "Are the rooms already paid for? Good, let's jet."

He peeked into the corridor before easing out into it. Han felt as tense as a wound spring as they rode down the drop shaft, but they encountered no trouble there or in the foyer. A robo-hack dropped them at one of the spaceport's side gates, a freighthauler's entrance near the *Falcon* that Han's shipmaster's credentials allowed him to use.

But when they reached the side of the approach opposite from the apron on which the *Falcon* was parked, Han suddenly yanked Fiolla back behind the shelter of a small orbital skiff and directed her attention to several loiterers in the area. "Recognize any of them?"

She frowned at them in the hazy sun. "Oh, you mean those goldskins? Aren't they the other swoop riders from this afternoon? But what are they doing here?"

He made an elaborate face at her. "They came to ask us to join their aerobatics club, what else?"

"What now?" Fiolla wanted to know.

Han took his macrobinoculars from their case at his side. Through them he could see Chewbacca moving around the cockpit of the *Millennium Falcon*, running a pre-flight check of the ship.

"At least Chewie's onboard," he told her, lowering the macros. "Spray and Bollux, too, I guess. Our friends are probably waiting for you and me to show up before they spring whatever they've got planned." Shooting their way out wouldn't work, he knew. Even if he and Fiolla could reach the *Falcon* under cover of her belly guns, their chances of evading the patrol network and picket ships overhead and making hyperspace would be almost nonexistent.

Fiolla held her lower lip between her teeth, pondering. "There are regular passenger connections between here and Ammuud; we could leave now, while they're watching your ship, and meet Chewbacca there. But how to let him know?"

Han looked up and down the rows of spacecraft on their side of the approach. "There's what we need," he said and, taking her hand, led her back through several rows of grounded vessels.

They came to the one Han had spotted, a large cargo lifter connected to a refueler, its outer access panels open. Han crawled up through an access panel and twenty seconds later threw open the small cockpit hatch.

"Nobody home," he told her as he gave her a hand up. Together they squeezed into the cramped cockpit. Han trained the macrobinoculars on his first mate across the way, and when the Wookiee chanced to look in his general direction, flashed the cargo lifter's running lights. Chewbacca took no notice.

It took four more tries to get the Wookiee's attention. Han saw his first mate's long, shaggy arm go to the console and the *Falcon*'s running lights blinked twice in acknowledgment.

Fiolla kept an eye on those individuals watching the *Falcon* to insure that they hadn't noticed what was going on. In so doing she spotted at least four more idlers mounting an inconspicuous guard on the freighter. Chewbacca pretended to be running a warmup while Han sent him a series of longs and shorts explaining their predicament and what the revised plan was. Throughout the process, Han was very aware of Fiolla pressed up against him in the confining cockpit; her perfume, he found, had a tendency to distract him.

When Han was finished, the *Falcon*'s lights blinked twice again. As he helped Fiolla down from the cargo lifter's cockpit hatch, a tech came up. "What were you people doing up there?"

Fiolla turned a scathing, imperious glare on the tech. "Is it now required that Port Safety overseers answer to ground crew? Well? Who's your supervisor?"

The tech murmured something apologetic, shuffling her feet and saying that she'd only been asking. Fiolla gave her one more haughty glare and departed with Han at her elbow. "And now we book passage out?" she asked once they had passed out of the tech's earshot.

"Yeah, I'll teach you all about getting offworld under a phony name. Chewie's going to stay put till we're clear, then lift off. They won't be expecting him to leave without us, so he shouldn't have any trouble. We will meet him on Ammuud."

"We're in luck," Fiolla said as she and Han stood studying the soaring holos that listed departures in the main passenger terminal. "There's a ship that goes straight to Ammuud, leaving this evening."

Han shook his head. "No, there's the one we want, departure 714, the shuttle."

Her brow furrowed. "But it's not even leaving this solar system."

"Which is why no one will be covering it," he countered. "They're likely to have watchers on the through-ships. We can change ships and book passage for Ammuud at the first stop, it says in the index. Besides, the shuttle's leaving now, which appeals to me a whole lot more. We'll have to hurry."

They tried not to appear too anxious as they bought tickets and barely made it to the departure gate in time. Since the ship was only an inter-system shuttle, it offered no sleeping accommodations beyond big, comfortable acceleration chairs. Han buckled himself in and let his chair back, sighing and preparing to drop off to sleep.

Fiolla had grabbed the window seat with no objection from Han. "Why did you make me pay for the tickets in cash?"

He opened one eye and studied her. "You want to
go around passing out Authority cash vouchers from
an open expense account? Good, go ahead; you might
as well hang a sign around your neck: AUTHORITY
EXEC—WON'T SOMEBODY PLEASE SHOOT ME?"

Her voice suddenly held a tremor. "Do, do you
think that's what's happened to Magg?"

He shut his eye again, lips tightening. "Absolutely
not; they'll hang on to him as a bargaining piece. All
I meant was that we don't want to leave a trail. Don't
pay any attention to me; sometimes I talk too much."

He could hear attempted cheer in her tone. "Or
you don't talk enough, Solo. I haven't decided which."
She settled herself to watch their liftoff. Han, who had
seen more of them than he'd ever be able to count,
was asleep before they left the troposphere.

At their destination, Roonadan, fifth planet out
from the same sun that warmed Bonadan, they discovered they had missed their starship connection.
The shuttle had been slightly delayed en route by in-
jector problems, but of course starships on interstellar
jump schedules are never held for mere interplanetary
traffic. They run on precise timetables for which hyperspace transitions are meticulously calculated in
advance by both onboard and ground-based computers. Straying from the strict timing of the jump
schedules was something the passenger lines hated to
do.

"But they don't mind leaving people stranded on
some rock," fumed Han, who had been known to calculate a hyperspace jump with one hand while dodg-
ing the law with a hold full of Kessel spice with the
other.

"Stop complaining. There's nothing we can do
about it," Fiolla reasoned. "There's another ship that
can get us to Ammuud, see? Departure 332."

He checked the holo listings. "Are you crazy? That's
an M-class ship, probably a tour. Look at that, they're

going to stop at two, no, three other planets. And they're not exactly going to be burning up hyperspace either."

"It's the quickest way to Ammuud," Fiolla said sensibly. "Or would you rather go back and try to make peace with the people who were chasing us all over Bonadan? Or wait for them to trace us here?"

Han was painfully aware that Chewbacca and the *Millennium Falcon* would be waiting on Ammuud. "Uh, I don't suppose you have enough cash to charter a ship of our own without using a voucher?"

She smiled at him sweetly. "Why yes, growing right here off my petty-cash vine; I was saving up the harvest until I had enough to buy my own fleet. Try to be rational, will you, Solo?"

"All right, lay off. At least it won't cost us more than a few Standard timeparts."

On the way to the reservations deck they passed travelers from dozens of worlds. There were wobbly-fleshed Courataines in their exoskeletal travel suits, breathing the thinnest of atmospheres through their respirators; octopedal Wodes, heavy-stepping and unused to less than two Standard gravities; beautifully plumed Jastáals trilling their phrases to one another as they half-glided along, wings partially extended; and human beings in all their variety.

A hand dropped onto Han's shoulder. He started, pivoting with a blurringly fast motion that freed him of the hand, put distance between himself and the other, and brought his right hand down to where his blaster would ordinarily have been.

"Easy, Han; old reflexes die hard, I see," laughed the man who had stopped him. Braced to confront Zlarb's business associates or a flying squad of Espos, Han felt abrupt relief not unmixed with a new worry as he recognized the man.

"Roa! What are you doing here?" Roa had put on weight, too much of it, but it didn't conceal the open, friendly features of one of the best smugglers and blockade-runners Han had ever known.

Roa smiled, looking as pleasantly paternal and trustworthy as ever. "Passing through, just like everyone else, son, and I thought I recognized you." Roa was carrying an expensive command case, a compact, self-contained business office. He wore a conservative beige suit with soft white shoes and rainbow girthsash. "You remember Lwyll, I'm sure."

The woman introduced by Roa had been standing to one side. Now she came forward. "How's it been with you, Han?" she asked in that rich voice he recalled so well. Lwyll hadn't gone as far to flesh as her husband; she was still a striking woman with masses of wavy white-blond hair and an elegant face. Han thought that she certainly didn't look—how many Standard years older?

Seeing them brought back a surge of memory of the fast, furious time he had spent working for Roa, when he had tired of trying to be just one more honest, unassuming spacer a few credits away from poverty, like uncounted others wandering the stars, having abandoned a planet and a life.

It had been Roa who had taken Han on his first exhilarating, harrowing Kessel Run—very nearly his last. In Roa's organization Han had risen quickly with a reputation for taking mad chances, daring any odds, running fearsome risks in the pursuit of illegal profit.

But they had parted company a long time ago, and honor among thieves was a more romantic myth than a dependable institution. Han's immediate reaction on seeing Roa was pleasure, but close on its heels was suspicion that this wasn't altogether an accident. Could word be out already, carrying a price on Han's head, through the interstellar underworld?

Still, Roa showed no sign of hailing the Espos. Fiolla cleared her throat, and Han made introductions. Roa waved at Han's lack of gunbelt. "So you're out of the game, too, eh? Well, I don't blame you, Han. Bowed out myself, just after we parted company. Lwyll and I had one close call too many. And, after all, doing business isn't too unlike our old line of work. A background in felony can be a real plus. What's your new line of endeavor?"

"A collections agency. Han Solo Associates, Limited."

"Ah? Sounds like your ideal; you always fought for what you had coming. How's your old sidekick, the Wook? Do you ever see any of the others? Tregga maybe, or even Vonzel?"

"Tregga's doing life at hard labor on Akrit'tar; they caught him before he could dump a load of *chak*-root. Sonniod's running a delivery service, living hand to mouth. The Briil twins are dead; they shot it out with a patrol cruiser out in the Tion Hegemony. And Vonzel messed up an emergency landing; most of what's left of him will be in a life-support clinic for good. He started a regular one-man run on the organ banks."

Roa shook his head sadly. "Yes, I'd forgotten how the deck is stacked. Few make it, Han."

He came back to the present. Squaring his shoulders, he dipped two fingers into his gaudy sash and drew out a business card. "Fifth largest import-export firm in this part of space," he boasted. "We've got some of the best tax-and-tariff men in the business. Drop around one of these days, and we'll talk over old times."

Han tucked away the card. Roa had turned to his wife. "I'll see that our baggage is transferred. You make sure our shuttle reservation's confirmed, my dear." He looked wistful for a moment. "We're lucky to be out of it, aren't we, Han?"

"Yeah, Roa, we sure are." The older man clapped him on the shoulder, made a polite leave-taking to Fiolla, and marched away.

Lwyll, waiting until her husband was gone, gave Han a knowing, amused look. "You're not out of it at all, are you, Han? No, I can tell; not Han Solo. Thanks for not telling him." Lwyll touched his cheek once and left.

"You've got interesting friends," was Fiolla's only comment, but her perspective on him had changed. Youthful looks belied the fact that he was a survivor in a calling with a very high rate of attrition.

Watching Roa's retreating back, Han thought about tax-and-tariff men and fingered the business card. "Solo, hey, wake up!" Fiolla assailed him. "It's our necks we're supposed to be preoccupied with here."

He sauntered off toward the interstellar reservations desks. *Things could be worse,* Han reflected.

"Bugging your eyes out at them won't help," said Fiolla, referring to the gambling tables and other games of chance in the swank wagering compartment just off the passenger liner's main salon.

She was wearing a sheer, clinging gown and soft evening slippers of polychromatic shimmersilk. She had brought the outfit with her, packed away in her upper-right thigh pouch and lower-left calf stuffpocket, on the assumption that her coveralls would do for all but the most formal places. She wore it now for a change of pace and a morale booster. Han still wore his ship clothes, but had closed his collar.

"We could go over what we know so far," she proposed.

"That's all we've been doing since we came onboard," he grimaced.

That wasn't entirely true. They had spoken of any number of things during the trip; he found her a spirited and amusing companion, much more so than any of the other passengers, aside from a frustrating tendency to keep her stateroom door locked during the liner's "night." But they had exchanged stories.

For instance, Fiolla had explained to him how she and her assistant, Magg, had been doing an audit on Bonadan when her portable command-retrieval computer terminal malfunctioned. She had turned to Magg's, which, having a more comprehensive cybernetic background, was a more complicated instrument with a number of keyboard differences. Some miskeying or accident had opened up a restricted informational pocket in Bonadan's system. There she had found records of the slavery ring's activities and the notation of Zlarb's impending payoff.

Han's eyes were still riveted to players trying their luck or skill at Point Five, Bounce, Liar's Cut, Vector, and a half-dozen other games. For two Standard timeparts, ever since coming aboard the passenger liner *Lady of Mindor,* he had been trying to come up with a way to get into a game. Now that he was completely rested, inactivity was nearly intolerable.

Fiolla had absolutely refused to back him, though Han had promised bountiful returns on her investment. He then pointed out that if she hadn't squandered money on separate accommodations, she would have had plenty to loan him.

"I didn't have time to brush up on my hand-to-hand," had been her retort. "And besides, if you're such a good gambler, how come you're flying around in that cookie-box freighter instead of a star yacht?"

He changed the subject. "We've been on this mud cart for two Standard timeparts. To get to Ammuud! No wonder I'm going crazy; the *Falcon* could've gotten us there in the time it took these idiots to clear port."

He rose from the little table where they had eaten an indifferent meal. "At least we'll make planetfall soon. Maybe I'll go run my clothes through the robovalet one more time for fun."

She caught his wrist. "Don't be so depressed. And please don't leave me here alone; I'm afraid that

priest of Ninn will corner me for another lecture on
the virtues of formalistic abstinence. And no com-
ments! Come on, I'll play you a game of Starfight.
That we can afford."

Not many passengers remained in the lounge, for
the *Lady of Mindor* was due to reenter normal space
shortly; most of them were packing or making other
last-minute preparations. He gave in and they crossed
to the bank of coin games.

She mimicked his rangy walk, swaggering along
next to him, arms dangling a bit and shoulders
slumped back. There was an exaggerated sway to her
hips as she swept the room arrogantly with narrowed
eyes and an invisible blaster weighting her side, right
in step with him.

When he noticed, he recognized himself at once. He
glared around the salon in case anyone was inclined to
laugh. "Will you quit that?" he said out of the side of
his mouth. "Somebody's liable to call you out."

She chuckled. "Then they'll stop a blaster bolt,
handsome; I've been studying with the master." He
found himself laughing, as she'd intended.

The Starfight game consisted of two curved banks
of monitors and controls, almost surrounding each of
the two playing stations. Between them was a large
holotank with detailed star charts. With the stacks
and stacks of controls, each player sent his myriad
ships out to do battle in computer modeled deepspace.

He stopped her as she was about to drop a coin into
the game. "I've never been too partial to Starfight,"
he explained. "It's too much like work."

"What about a last stroll through the promenade?"

It was as good a diversion as any. They ascended
the curved staircase to find they had the promenade to
themselves. The novelty of the place must have worn
off for the other passengers. A single pane of transparisteel ten meters long and five high curved to fol-

low the ship's hull, showing them the tangled luminosity of hyperspace. They stared with the age-old fascination, their human minds and eyes trying to impose order on the chaos beyond the transparisteel so that, at times, they believed they saw shapes, surfaces, or fluxes.

She noticed he was still distracted. "You're thinking about Chewie, aren't you?"

A shrug. "He'll be all right. I just hope the big lug didn't worry himself sick when we were overdue and start shedding or something."

The ship's public-address system announced final warning of transition, though it was for crew members rather than passengers. Shortly thereafter Fiolla pointed and breathed a soft exclamation as the distortions and discord of hyperspace melted away and they gazed out at a field of stars. Due to the liner's position they could see neither Ammuud nor its primary.

"How long to—" Fiolla was saying, when emergency klaxons began hooting all through the ship. The lighting flickered and died and was replaced by far dimmer emergency illumination. The outcries of frightened passengers could be heard as distant echoes in the passageways.

"What's happening?" Fiolla yelled over the din. "A drill?"

"It's no drill," he said. "They've shut down everything but emergency systems; they must be channeling power into their shields."

He grabbed her hand and started back for the staircase. "Where are we going?" she hollered.

"The nearest escape-pod station or lifeboat bay," was his shouted answer.

The salon was deserted. As they got into the passageway the entire liner rocked under them. Han recovered with the agility of a seasoned spacer, keeping

his balance and stopping Fiolla just before she collided
with a bulkhead.

"We've been hit!" he called. As if to underscore
what he said, they heard massive airtight doors sliding
into place automatically throughout the ship. The *Lady
of Mindor* had taken hull damage of some sort and
been breached.

A steward came running down the passageway with
a medipack under one arm. When Han saw he wasn't
about to stop, he grabbed a double handful of the
man's heavily braided jacket.

"Let go," the steward said, trying to twist free.
"You're supposed to proceed to your quarters. All
passengers proceed to quarters."

Han shook him. "First tell me what's going on!"

"Pirates! They shot out the main drive as soon as we
made transition from hyperspace!" The news shocked
Han so much that he released his grip.

As he ran off on his way, the steward shouted back
at them. "Return to your quarters, you fools! We're
being boarded!"

VII

"THIS vessel is a fraud," Spray announced, keying his next move into the gameboard in the *Millennium Falcon*'s forward compartment.

Chewbacca took just enough time from what he was doing—analyzing Spray's unorthodox stratagem—to snarl threateningly.

Spray, who had grown more used to the Wookiee's outbursts, didn't flinch much at all. He was dividing his time between the compartment's technical station and the gameboard, giving the *Falcon*'s first mate a very difficult match while running a combination inventory and inspection of the ship out of a sense of duty to Interstellar Collections Limited. Chewbacca permitted it more to keep the skip-tracer busy than anything else, but this slandering of the *Falcon*, if unchecked, could only lead to retribution.

Come to think of it, the Wookiee reflected, *the Tynman wasn't a bad technical pilot.* He had even assisted on the liftoff from Bonadan, once Chewbacca had judged that Han and Fiolla had won enough time to get offworld. Spray had copiloted and aided in hyperspace transition with a fussy proficiency, though he'd been startled to learn that Han and Chewbacca habitually spaced by themselves, Han reaching back to his left to carry out navigator's chores and the Wookiee leaning to his right to run the commo board when needed.

"The exterior is a deception," Spray was continuing.

"Why, some of the equipment you've installed is restricted to military use; are you aware of that? And
her armament rating's way too high, as is her lift/mass
ratio. How did Captain Solo ever get a waiver to operate within the Authority?"

The Wookiee, cupping his hirsute chin in both hands,
leaned down even closer to the gameboard, ignoring
the question. Even if he had been able to communicate eloquently with Spray, he wouldn't have explained
about the waiver, which had involved an amazing variety of lawbreaking and the total destruction of the
covert Authority facility known as Stars' End.

Miniature holomonsters waited on the circular
gameboard, throwing challenges to one another. Chewbacca's defenses had been penetrated by a lone combatant from Spray's forces. The question of external
versus internal threat was a very subtle one, involving
closely matched win/lose parameters. The Wookiee's
nose scrunched in thought. He reached a hairy finger
out very slowly and punched his next move up on the
game's keyboard, then reclined on the curving acceleration couch, arm pillowing his head, his long legs
crossed. With his free hand he scratched his other
arm, which the somatigenerative effect of the flaking
synthflesh had made itchy.

"Uh-oh," blurted Blue Max, who was following the
contest from his habitual place in Bollux's open thorax.
The 'droid sat on a pressure keg among the other clutter to one side of the compartment, amid plastic pal-
lets, hoisting toggles and a rebuilt fuel enricher that
Han hadn't gotten around to installing yet. The computer probe's photoreceptor swiveled to track on Spray
as the Tynnan returned to the board and made his
next move without hesitation.

Spray's lone combatant had been a decoy. Now one
of his supporting monsters slithered across the board
and, after a brief battle, threw Chewbacca's defenses
wide open.

"It's the eighth Ilthmar gambit; he drew you out with that loner. He's got you," Blue Max observed helpfully.

Chewbacca was filling his lungs for a vituperative outpouring and levering himself up to the board again when the navicomputer clamored for attention. The starship's first mate forgot his ire and scrambled up from the acceleration couch, but not before he cleared the board of his humiliating defeat. He hastened off to prepare for the reversion to normal space.

"And just look at this; some of these systems are fluidic!" Spray squeaked after him, whiskers aquiver, waving a tech readout screen. "What is this, a starship or a distillery?"

The Wookiee paid him no heed. "Good game, Spray," attested Max, who was himself a fair player.

"He held me for three extra moves," admitted the skip-tracer. "I wish things were going as well with this technical survey. Everything's so modified that I can't trace the basic specifications."

"Maybe we can help," Max piped brightly.

"Max *is* conversant with ship's systems," Bollux said. "He might be able to dig out the information you require."

"Just what I need! Please, step over to the tech station!" Spray was behind the 'droid, webbed feet scrabbling on the deckplates, pushing him to a seat at the station. As Bollux sat heavily into the acceleration chair, Max extended an adaptor, the one Chewbacca had repaired after the encounter with the slavers.

"I'm in," Max announced as technical readouts began marching across scopes and screens at high speed. "What d'you want to know, Spray?"

"All data on recent jumps; you can patch into the navi-computer. I want to see how the ship's been operating."

"You mean accuracy factors and power levels?" Max asked in his childish voice.

"I mean hyperspace jumps, date-time coordinates, all relevant information. It'll give me the simplest evaluation of how the ship performs and what she's worth."

There was a momentary hesitation. "It's no use," Max told Spray. "Captain Solo's got all that stuff protected. He and Chewbacca are the only ones with access."

Exasperated, Spray pursued. "Can't you find a window to it? I thought you were a computer probe."

Max achieved a wounded tone. "I *am*. But I can't do something like this without the Captain's permission. Besides, if I make a mistake, the safeguards will wipe everything clean."

As the Tynnan sat and stewed, Bollux drawled, "As I understand it, a general examination would begin with things like power systems, maintenance records, and so forth. Would you like Blue Max to run a thorough check of current status?"

Spray seemed distracted. "Eh? Oh, yes, yes, that would be fine." Then he sat, bucktoothed chin poised on a stubby paw, stroking his whiskers in concentration.

"Whoops," chirped Max, "what d'you suppose *that* is? Whatever it is wasn't there when we did the preflight warmup."

The skip-tracer suddenly became attentive. "What are you—oh, that power drop? Hm, that's a minor conduit on the outer hull, isn't it? Now what could be draining power there?"

"Nothing in design schematics or mod-specs," Max assured him. "I think we should tell Chewbacca."

Spray, never one to trust the unexplained, was inclined to agree. Yielding to the skip-tracer's nervous exhortations, the Wookiee left the cockpit only under protest, and seated himself at the tech station. But when he saw evidence of the highly improbable power drain, his thick red-gold brows beetled and his leathery nostrils dilated reflexively, trying to catch a whiff of what was wrong.

He turned and brayed an interrogative at Spray, who had been around the Wookiee long enough to understand that much.

"I haven't a clue," the skip-tracer answered stridently. "Nothing in this slapdash ship makes any sense to me. She looks like a used loadlifter, but she's got higher boost than an Imperial cruiser. I don't even care to think about how jury-rigged some of those reroutings must be."

At Chewbacca's order Blue Max showed him, on a computer model, exactly which length of the conduit was experiencing drainage. The Wookiee marched to the tool locker, withdrew a worklight, a scanner and a huge spanner, and continued on aft with Spray and Bollux bringing up the rear.

Near the engine shielding, the *Falcon*'s first mate removed a wide inspection plate and wormed himself down into the crawlspace there. He had even less room than normal—a good deal of the fluidic systems had been installed here.

He barely managed to turn his wide shoulders and squeeze the scanner in by the hull. He played its invisible tracer beam over the metal, watching the monitor carefully. At last he found the spot where, on the other side of the hull, the power conduit was showing droppage. It didn't look like any malfunction he had ever seen; there should be no reason for the conduit simply to lose power. Something must be drawing it from the conduit, but Chewbacca could think of nothing that would do so. Unless, of course, something had been added.

In a moment he was wriggling his way back out of the crawlspace like an enormous red-gold-brown larva, honking his distress. Bollux's vocoder and Max's vied with Spray's high-strung squeak, demanding to know what was wrong. Sweeping them out of his way with

one wide swing of his arm, Chewbacca headed for the
storage compartment where his oversized spacesuit was
stored.

The Wookiee detested the confinement of a suit and
loathed even more the idea of clambering along the
hull and undertaking delicate and dangerous work
while protected from the annihilation of hyperspace
only by the thin envelope of the *Falcon*'s drive field.
But more than that he dreaded what he believed he
would find on the other side of the hull.

The decision was taken out of his hands. There was
a loud *ploow!* Out of the still-open inspection port
came a burst of flame and explosive force along with
gasses and vaporized liquids from the fluidic components. There followed a sustained whistle of air that
let them know the vessel had been holed, confirming
the Wookiee's worst fears. During the ground-time on
Bonadan, someone, most probably the enemies waiting for Han and Fiolla, had taken precautionary measures to insure that the *Millennium Falcon* wouldn't
escape. They had fastened a sleeper-bomb to the
starship's hull where it would do the worst damage. It
had been applied inert, unpowered, undetectable except by the most minute inspection. Once in flight it had
become active, draining power from the ship's systems
to build its explosion. Then it had released in a shaped
charge and blown out control systems in flight. The device was meant to produce the cleanest possible kind
of murder, one that would leave no evidence, blasting
the ship and all it contained into meaningless energy
anomalies in hyperspace.

Chewbacca and Spray were driven back by the
multicolored reek belching from the ruptured fluidics.
Unprotected, they could be killed as easily by breathing those concentrated gases as by a miscalculated
transition.

But Bollux could get along quite well where they
couldn't. They saw the 'droid clank through the bil-

lowing smoke, lugging a heavy extinguisher he had
pulled from a wall niche. Chewbacca had occasion now
to curse the same auto-firefighting gear that had saved
them all on Lur; the system's inability to operate now
might spell their deaths.

Bollux's chest panels closed protectively over
Blue Max even as he set the extinguisher down and
lowered himself stiffly into the crawlspace, his gleaming
body poorly suited to an area designed for limber living creatures. Once he had entered the space, his
lengthy arm reached back out to drag the extinguisher
after him. There was still the shriek of escaping air and
the *whoop* of warning sirens to tell them the *Falcon*
was depressurizing.

Chewbacca had run for the cockpit with Spray
crowding behind. At the control console he kicked in
filtration systems full-all, to carry away toxic fumes,
and checked damage indicators.

The bomb must have been relatively small, placed
in a precise location by someone who knew stock
freighters like the *Falcon* well. The Wookiee realized
it before Spray—whoever had planted the sleeper-
bomb hadn't been aware of the starship's tread-
boarded fluidics setup. With the control design
radically altered, the bomb had failed to do a complete
job of rendering the starship derelict.

Transition to normal space was imminent. Without
taking time to seat himself, Chewbacca reached over
his seat and worked at the console. At least some of
the fluidics were functioning; hyperspace parted around
the freighter like an infinite curtain.

The *Falcon*'s first mate bellowed an angry imprecation at the Universe's sense of timing, picked Spray
up bodily and deposited him in the pilot's seat, bayed
a string of uninterpreted instructions while pointing at
the planet Ammuud, which had just appeared before
them, and tore off in the direction of the explosion.

He paused long enough to pick up a hull-patch

kit and a respirator. Hunkering down over the inspection plate, he saw Bollux sitting in the midst of shards and fragments of fluidic tubing and microfilament. The fire had been quelled. The shriek of escaping air had stopped: Bollux had firmly planted his durable back against the breach, an adequate sort of temporary seal.

The labor 'droid looked up and was relieved to see Chewbacca. "The hole is rather large, sir; I'm not sure how long my thorax will withstand the pressure. Also, the armor surrounding the breach is cracked. I suggest using the largest patch you have."

Chewbacca analyzed the thorny problem of getting Bollux out of the crawlspace and simultaneously plugging the hole. He settled on the plan of preparing two patches, one smaller and lighter that could be set in place quickly, and the other a sturdy plate that would hold up even against the massive force exerted by the *Falcon*'s air pressure toward the utter vacuum outside. He handed the smaller patch down to Bollux and yipped instructions, gesturing to make himself understood, frustrated that he'd never mastered Basic.

But the 'droid grasped what he meant and gathered himself for the effort. Using the agility of his special suspension system and his simian arms, Bollux managed to push himself free, swing around, and slap the patch into place in rapid sequence. He swarmed for the inspection opening, having seen that the temporary patch was trembling before the strain placed upon it.

Chewbacca had seen it, too, and worried; the hole was bigger than he had thought. He reached down with both arms and hauled the 'droid up through the inspection opening. Just as he did the patch gave way, sucked into nothingness so quickly that it seemed to vanish. With it went several jagged pieces, enlarging the hole.

It was suddenly as if Chewbacca was standing in the middle of a wild river-rapids, fighting raging currents of air that, in escaping the ship, were dragging him inexorably toward the hole. Scraps and loose debris swirled around and past him and zipped down the inspection opening.

Bracing the muscular columns of his legs on either side of the opening, the Wookiee fought to retain his hug on Bollux and resist that flood. The giant sinew of his back and legs felt as if it were about to come apart. He clutched the 'droid to him with one arm, bracing the other on the deck, sustaining himself on a tripod of arm and legs, head thrown back with effort.

Bollux recovered somewhat, only to find that in the position in which the Wookiee was holding him, he could do little to exert any force of his own. What he could and did do was grasp the corner of the inspection plate and swing it over on its pivot, something Chewbacca hadn't a free limb to accomplish. It almost jammed halfway, but with a final tug the 'droid cleared it. Once it was past that point the airflow caught it and hauled it shut with a ringing slam. Fortunately none of the Wookiee's fingers or toes were poised on the lip of the opening.

The depressurization was confined to one small compartment for the time being. How serious that was remained to be seen. Chewbacca wanted to lie on the deck and catch his breath for a moment but knew he didn't have the time. He squirted thick, gluey sealant all around the inspection plate, then paused long enough to pat Bollux's cranium with a gruff compliment.

"It was Max who brought the inspection plate to my attention," said the 'droid modestly. Then he hauled himself to his feet and trailed off after Chewbacca, who had already dashed off toward the cockpit.

There, Spray was engaged in an uncertain contest with the controls. "We retain considerable guidance function," he reported, "and I've put us on an approach path to the planet's only spaceport. I was about to alert them for an emergency landing under crash conditions."

The Wookiee loudly countermanded that plan, dropping into his outsized copilot seat. He, like Han, shunned involvement, and the consequent fuss or furor, that could possibly be avoided. He found that the controls responded adequately and thought he stood a good chance of landing the freighter without sirens, crash wagons, stop-netting, firefighting robos, and ten thousand official questions.

Already in Ammuud's upper atmosphere, he brought the ship onto a steady approach path. Her hyperspace drive seemed to have suffered damage, but the rest of her guidance system responded within tolerance.

Bollux, who had just caught up, came up next to Chewbacca, his panels open. "I think there's something you should know, sir. Blue Max just ran a quick check at the tech station. The damage has stabilized, but some of the filament tubing for the guidance systems has been exposed; its housing was cracked."

"Will it blow?" Spray asked. Below them, they could make out features of the terrain quite clearly. Ammuud was a world of immense forests and oceans with rather large polar ice caps.

Max answered. "It's not a question of blowing *out,* Spray; they're secure, but they're delicate low-pressure filaments. Going too deep into the planet's atmosphere will implode them."

"You mean we can't land?" Spray blinked.

"No," Bollux replied calmly. "He merely means that we can't land too deep in Ammuud's—"

The starship gave a convulsive shudder.

"Be careful!" squawked the skip-tracer to Chewbacca. "This vessel is still in lien to Interstellar Collections Limited!"

Chewbacca gave out a vociferous growl. One of the control filaments had imploded, the planet's atmosphere having overcome the lesser pressure within it.

The Wookiee snarled. Working to bypass the line, he had one bit of luck in that he could cut the ship's speed back to a very gentle descent.

"—atmosphere," Bollux finished.

"How deep is that?" Spray asked urgently. The Terrain Following Sensors had already shown them the planet's spaceport at the foot of a high mountain range.

"Not very much lower at all, sir," commented Bollux in neutral tones.

The Wookiee pulled the *Falcon*'s bow higher and reset the Terrain Following Sensors to display the features of the mountain range beyond Ammuud's spaceport. His plan was clear; since he couldn't set down in the lower atmosphere, he would find as suitable a site as he could in the higher mountains and hope that the lower air pressure there wouldn't collapse the rest of the guidance system before he could set the ship down. He waved a shaggy paw at Bollux and Spray, indicating the passageway.

"I believe he wants us to stow all loose gear and prepare for a rough landing," Bollux told Spray. The two turned and began working their way along the passageway together, frantically cramming loose items into storage lockers and securing their lids.

They had reached the escape pods when Spray thought of something important. "What about Captain Solo? How will he know what's happened?"

"I'm afraid I can't say, sir," Bollux confessed. "I see no way in which we can safely leave word for him without compromising ourselves to port officials."

The skip-tracer accepted that. "By the way, I think there's some welding equipment in that second pod there; you'd better bring it out so that we can secure it."

Bollux obligingly leaned into the open pod. "I don't see any—" He felt an abrupt push from behind. Spray had worked up just enough momentum, with a running start, so that shoving with all his might he toppled Bollux into the pod.

"Find Solo!" Spray yelled, and hit the release. Inner and outer hatches rolled down before the confused 'droid could get out another word. The pod was blown free by its separator charges.

And as the *Falcon* nosed up, driving for the high mountains of Ammuud, the dumpy escape pod began its fall toward the spaceport.

VIII

GENERAL Quarters or any call to stations can be
disorderly in even a well-run military spacecraft. On a
passenger liner like the *Lady of Mindor,* where run-
throughs and practices were all but ignored, it was
total confusion. Therefore, Han Solo paid scant attention to the garbled and frequently contradictory instructions blared by the public-address annunciators.
With Fiolla in tow he plunged down the passageway as
panicky passengers, frightened crew members, and in-
decisive officers immobilized one another with con-
flicting aims and actions.

"What are you going to do?" Fiolla asked as they
sidestepped a mob of passengers hammering at the
purser's door.

"Get the rest of your cash from your stateroom,
then find the nearest lifeboat bay." He heard airtight
doors booming shut and tried to remember the layout of
these old M-class ships. It would be disastrous to be
trapped by the automatic seal-up.

"Solo, *tractor in!*" Fiolla bawled, dragged her slip-
pered feet, and finally halted him. Catching her breath,
she continued. "I have my money with me. Unless you
want to tip the robo-valet, we can get going."

He was once again impressed. "Very good. We keep
going aft; there should be a boat just forward of the
power section." He recalled that his macrobinoculars
were back in his cabin, then wrote them off. Ahead of
them an airtight door had just begun grinding shut.

They made it in a sprint, though the hem of Fiolla's shimmersilk caught in the hatchway and she had to tear a ragged edge off it to free herself.

"A month's pay, this thing cost me," she complained ruefully. "What's it going to be now, fight or run?"

"A little of both. The fool captain of this can must've tripped every door in the ship. How does he think his crew'll get to battle stations?" He started on.

"Maybe he doesn't intend to fight," she puffed, staying right at his heels. "I hardly think a liner's crew could make a fight of it against a pirate, do you?"

"They'd better; pirates aren't famous for their restraint with captives." They came to a long, cylindrical lifeboat tucked into its bay. Han broke the seal on the release lever and threw it back, but the lifeboat's hatch failed to roll open. He threw the lever forward and back again, condemning the liner's maintenance officer for not looking after his safety equipment.

"Listen," Fiolla stopped him.

The ship's captain seemed to have reasserted a certain amount of self-control. "For the safety of all passengers," his voice came from the PA, "and crew members alike, I've decided to accept terms of surrender offered by the vessel that disabled us. I have been assured that no one will be harmed so long as we put up no resistance and no attempt is made to launch lifeboats. With this in mind I have overridden boat and pod releases to keep them onboard. Though the ship is damaged, we are in no immediate danger. I hereby order all passengers and crew members to cooperate with the boarding parties when the pirate craft docks with ours."

"What makes him think they'll keep their word?" Han muttered. "He's been larding it on passenger runs too long." A small part of him chased after that thought. When *was* the last time a pirate raid had been made near the well-patrolled inner environs of the

Authority? An attack of this sort was nearly unheard of in this part of space.

"Solo, look!" Fiolla pointed to an open hatch, this one set into the liner's outer hull. He ran to it and found that it gave access to a gun turret. The hatch had obviously opened at the first alarm. The twin-barreled blaster cannon was unattended; either its assigned crew hadn't made it to their station or the captain had recalled them.

Hiking himself through the hatch, Han settled into the gunner's saddle as Fiolla lowered herself into the gunner's mate's place. Through the blister of transpari-steel enclosing the turret they could see the pirate craft, a slender predator painted in light-absorbing black, warping in adroitly on the passenger liner. The pirate was apparently going to match up against an airlock in the *Lady*'s midsection somewhat forward of the gun turret.

The emplacement was fully charged. Setting his shoulders against the rests, Han leaned against the padded hood of the targeting scope, closing his hands on the firing grips.

"What've you got in mind, Solo?" Fiolla queried sharply.

"If we start maneuvering the turret, they'll pick the movement up," he explained. "But if we wait, they will drift right across our sights. We can get off one volley, maybe even disable them."

"Maybe even get ourselves killed," she suggested tartly. "And everybody else into the bargain. Solo, you can't!"

"Wrong; it's the one thing I *can* do. Do you think they'll keep their word about not hurting anyone? I don't. We can't escape, but we sure can take a swipe at them."

Ignoring her protests, he put his shoulders to the rests and sighted through the targeting scope again. The pirate's menacing shape came into the edge of his field of fire. He held his breath, waiting for a shot at the raider's vitals, knowing he would get off only one salvo.

The control section didn't quite come into his line of fire and he let the crew quarters pass; they were probably empty, with most of the crew mustered at the airlock for boarding. The pirate wouldn't even have to put out her boats, thanks to the liner captain's meek surrender.

Han peered through the scope at the next length of enemy hull, then pushed himself away from the twin cannon and began drawing himself headfirst out of the gunner's saddle. "Let's go," he prompted Fiolla.

"What's this, the sudden onset of senile sanity?"

"Inspiration's my specialty," he replied lightly. "I just hope I remember the layout of this old M-class right. It's a long time since I shipped in one."

She trailed him forward again as he studied engineer's markings on the liner's frames, talking to himself under his breath. There quickly followed the hollow, heavy concussion of the pirate making fast to the liner's hull. Han skidded to a stop and drew Fiolla back into the temporary safety of a side passageway.

Not too far ahead a covey of passengers had foolishly gathered near a main airlock in defiance of the captain's instructions. Among them Fiolla recognized the priest of Ninn in his green vestments, an Authority assistant supervisor of plant innoculation from an agroworld, and a dozen others she had come to know. All of them shrank back from the pneumatic sounds of the airlock's cycling.

Then the passengers rushed away like game-avians flushed from cover as the airlock's inner hatch swung open and armed boarders poured into the passageway. The boarders, wearing armored spacesuits, brandished blasters, force-pikes, rocket launchers, and vibro-axes. They had the look of faceless, invulnerable executioners.

There were orders from helmet speaker grilles and cries from the passengers. The latter were ignored amid a great deal of rough handling. A takeover team dashed toward the *Lady*'s bridge with shock grenades, fusion-cutters, plasma torches, and sapper charges, in case the captain changed his mind about surrendering. A few of the boarders began herding feebly objecting passengers toward the lounge while the rest split up into teams and began a rapid search outward in all directions from the airlock.

Han led Fiolla to an inboard passageway and struck out aft again, still reading frame markings, until they came to a utility locker. Inside the locker was a hatch giving access to a service core that ran the length of the ship. Normally the hatch would have been secured shut, but it could, for safety's sake, be opened manually when the ship was on emergency status. Han undogged it and entered the service core, squatting among power conduits and thick cables. Ventilation was never good in these cores, and layers of dust had settled everywhere, deposited by the liner's wheezy circulators.

Fiolla made a face. "What good's hiding? We're liable to wind up adrift in a derelict, Solo."

"We've got a reservation for two on the next boat out of here. Now get in; you're letting in a draft."

She entered awkwardly, trailing skirt gathered in one hand, and climbed under him so that he could dog the hatch, then clumsily shifted position to let him lead the way. He noticed, in the process, that Fiolla had two very nice legs.

The trip soon had both of them dirty, hot, and irritable as they hauled themselves over, under, and between obstacles. "Why is life so complicated around you?" she panted. "The pirates would take my money and leave me in peace, but not Han Solo, oh no!"

He sniggered nastily as he loosened the clips on a

grating and wrenched it out of his way. "Has it occurred to you yet that this isn't a pirate attack?"

"I wouldn't know; I get invited to so few of them."

"Trust me; it's not. And they sure could've found fat-
ter, safer targets out in the fringe areas. They're taking
an awful risk hitting this close to Espo patrols. And
then there's all this nonsense about not launching the
boats. They're after someone in particular, and I think
it's us."

He was leading her in a strained, squatting progress
over ducts and power routing, bumping heads on the
occasional low-hanging conduit. There were only inter-
mittent emergency lights, nodes that only slightly relieved the darkness. After what seemed like an
eternity he found the hatch he had been searching
for, just aft of a major reinforced frame.

"Where are we?" Fiolla asked.

"Just under and aft of the portside airlock," he said,
jerking his thumb toward the deck overhead. "The
Lady's probably swarming with boarders by now."

"Then what're we doing here? Has anyone ever criti-
cized your leadership, Solo?"

"Never ever." He ascended a short ladder and she
followed dubiously. But when he tried the hatch at
the top he found its valve frozen in place. Setting his
shoulder to its wheel and nearly losing his footing did
no more good.

"Here," Fiolla said, handing up a short length of
metal. He saw that she had pulled loose one of the
ladder rungs from beneath her.

"You're wasting your time doing honest work," he
told her frankly, and set the rung through the
wheel's spokes. The second try elicited a creaking of
metal and the wheel turned, then spun. He cracked
the hatch a fraction to have a look around and saw,
as he'd hoped he would, the interior of the utility
locker just off the airlock's inner hatch. In it hung the

maintenance ready-crew's spacesuits and tool harnesses, waiting to be donned on a moment's notice.

Drawing Fiolla up after him, he swung the core hatch shut as silently as he could. "There shouldn't be more than a guard or two out there at the airlock," he explained. "I doubt that they're worried about counterattack very much; there won't be more than two or three firearms onboard the *Lady* all told."

"Then what're we doing here?" She imitated his unconscious whisper.

"We can't hide for very long. If they have to, they'll sweep the whole ship with sensors, and I doubt that there are any shielded areas. There's only one place where we'll get an escape boat now."

She caught her breath as she realized what he meant and opened her mouth to object. But he put a finger across her lips. "They're slavers, not pirates, and they're not going through all this trouble just to let us live. They want to find out how much we know, then wipe our tapes for good. I'm not sure how this will work out, but if you get to the *Falcon* without me you can have Zlarb's data plaque. Tell Chewie it's in the breast pocket of my thermosuit and he'll know it's all right."

She started to say something, but he put her off. "Fight *and* run, remember? Here's what you do."

The guard watching the main airlock had been following the boarding via helmet comlink. The ship was fairly well secured and search parties were going through their assigned areas.

A noise from the utility locker attracted his attention. Though difficult to identify through the sound-dampening helmet, it sounded like metal striking metal.

Holding his launcher ready, the guard hit the hatch release. It swung the hatch out of the way and he entered the utility locker. At first he thought the room was empty; it had been searched earlier. But then he

noticed the figure crouching in a futile attempt to hide
behind one of the ready-crew's suits. It was a terrified
young woman wearing a torn evening gown.

The guard swung his weapon up at once and
checked out the rest of the locker, but it contained only
tools and hanging spacesuits. He stepped into the
locker, motioning with the launcher, switching to external address mode. "Come out of there right now and
I won't hurt you."

That turned out to be true in a way the guard
hadn't foreseen. A weighty power prybar caught him
across the helmet and shoulder, driving him to his
knees. Despite his armor the guard was stunned for a
moment and his shoulder and arm went numb. He fumbled for his comlink controls, but the blow had
smashed the transceiver on the side of his helmet.

The woman dashed up to try to wrench the launcher
away from him, but the guard fought to retain it. A
scrabbling sound from behind him and another clout
made the guard forget all about his weapon. Much of
the impact was absorbed by armor and helmet padding, but the blow had been so severe that even the
amount that penetrated knocked him out flat on his
face, dazed, with a huge dent in his helmet.

Han Solo, still in the spacesuit by which he'd dangled from a hook in ambush, threw himself on the
raider and quickly slipped a tool harness around him,
drawing it tight to pin his arms. With another he bound
the man's legs. Fiolla watched the entire process nervously, gazing at the shoulder-fired rocket launcher she
held as if it had materialized out of thin air.

Han rose and gently took the weapon from her. He
found it to be loaded with anti-personnel rounds,
flechette canisters. Those wouldn't hurt a boarder inside his armored spacesuit, but they'd be graphically
effective against unprotected passengers and crew
members. Han would have preferred a blaster, but the
old-fashioned launcher would suffice for now.

His voice was muted by the helmet he wore. "We don't know whether he's supposed to check in or what. All we can do is go. Ready?"

She tried to smile and he encouraged her with a grin. He closed the utility locker hatch behind him and in a moment they had crossed through the boarding tube and entered the raider craft.

The passageway there was empty. *They must have the whole panting pack out looking for us,* he thought.

Picturing the raider's hull as he had seen it when she'd warped in at the *Lady,* he started aft, heading for the boat bay that had made him stay his hand in the gun turret. He pushed Fiolla along in front of him and held the launcher at high port as if she were his prisoner. The spacesuit might keep him from being recognized as an outsider in the disorder of the boarding. It was, at least, worth a try.

He saw the caution lights and marker panels of a ship's boat bay ahead.

"You there! Halt!" he heard a voice behind him shout. He pretended not to hear, and gave Fiolla a shove on her way. But the voice repeated the command. "Halt!"

He spun on his cleated heel, brought the launcher up and found himself staring at a face he recognized. It was the black-haired man who had appeared in the message tape, the one who was to have met Zlarb. He and another man in armored spacesuits, helmets thrown back, were digging at their sidearms.

But the pistols were held in military-style holsters, built for durability rather than speed. *Might just as well have those guns home in a drawer,* Han reflected dispassionately as he aimed. Fiolla was screaming something he couldn't take time to listen to.

Both men realized at the last instant that they couldn't outshoot him and hurled themselves back, arms covering their faces, just as he fired.

The antipersonnel round was set for close work; the canister went off almost as soon as it left the launcher, boosting the flechettes and filling the passageway with a deafening concussion. The slavers didn't seem to be hurt, but remained on the deck where they had fallen. Han fired another AP round at them for good luck and, grabbing Fiolla's elbow, ran for the boat bay. She seemed to be in shock but didn't fight him. He opened the lock hatch and propelled her through.

"Find a place and grab on!" He found time to bite out a malediction that he had come upon a lifeboat rather than a pinnace or boarding craft.

A blaster beam mewed past him and burned out an illumination strip further down the passageway. Han knelt in the shelter of the lock and cut loose with four more rounds, emptying the launcher at the figures pounding down on him. They all dove for cover but he didn't think he had gotten any of them.

Closing both hatches, he threw himself into the boat's pilot's seat and detonated its separator charges. Unlike the liner's boats, the raider ships were still functioning. With a stupendous jolt the boat was blown from its lock. At the same moment he cut in full thrust and the lifeboat leaped as if it had been kicked.

Han swung hard, relying on steering thrusters alone here where there was no atmosphere to affect the tumbling boat's control surfaces. He piloted grimly to miss the liner's hull and looped up to put the bulk of the *Lady of Mindor* between himself and the slavers' vessel. Opening the boat's engine all the way, he vectored on until he was out of cannon range, then plunged toward the surface of Ammuud.

He freed one hand from his struggle long enough to fling back his helmet.

"Can we outrun them?" Fiolla asked from the acceleration chair behind him.

"There's more to it than that," he said without taking his eyes from the controls. "They can't come after us until they sound recall and get all their men back from the *Lady*. And if they want to send boats after us, they'd better have some awfully hot pilots."

He heard a lurching and, despite the pull of the boat's dive, Fiolla drew herself up to the copilot's chair. "Sit down and stay put," he told her heatedly, if a bit late. "If I'd had to maneuver or decelerate just then, you'd be scraping yourself off the bulkhead!"

She ignored that. He saw something else had so shocked her that she was still feeling the effect of it. Knowing how resilient she was ordinarily, he divided his attention for a moment.

"What's wrong? Besides the fact that we might be vaporized at any second, I mean."

"The man you shot at . . ."

"The black-haired one? He's the one who left the message I told you about; he was Zlarb's connection." He turned to her sharply. "Why?"

"It was Magg," Fiolla said, the blood drained from her face. "It was my hand-picked personal assistant, Magg."

IX

IT was early in the morning of Ammuud's short day when spaceport employees and automata alike stopped work as sirens announced a defense alert. Reinforced domes folded back to reveal emplacements around the port and in the snowy mountains above. For a quiet little spaceport, Ammuud's had an impressive array of weaponry.

A boat came out of the sky, catching the light. Its pilot hit braking thruster, and the ear-splitting sound of its passage caught up with it. Turbolasers, missile tubes, and multibarreled cannons traced its descent, eager to fire should the boat show the slightest sign of hostile action. The defense command was already aware that a brief ship-to-ship action had been fought above Ammuud, and they were inclined to take no chances. Interceptors were kept clear, since it was a lone craft, and the entire sky was a potential free-fire area.

But the boat set down obediently and precisely at one side of the field by port control, at a spot designated. Ground vehicles mounted with portable artillery closed in around the little vessel while the larger emplacements went back to standby. The spaceport automata, cargo-handlers, automovers, and the like, their simple circuitry satisfied that there was no reason to discontinue work, returned to their tasks, with one exception. No one even noticed the labor 'droid who, still carrying a shipping crate, started off across the field.

As he cracked the boat's hatch, Han turned to check on his companion. "Fiolla, you've got great judgment in hired help, that's all I can say."

"Solo, he passed an in-depth security investigation," she insisted, rather more loudly. "What was I supposed to do, have him brain-probed?"

Han stopped as he was about to swing down to the landing field. "Not a bad idea. Anyway, this tells us a lot. When you gained access to the slavers' computer pocket on Bonadan, it wasn't just because of miskeying. Magg's terminal probably had some sort of special-access equipment built into it; looks like he's the slavers' roving accountant, too, and maybe their security man as well.

"He sent you out on that scooter so you could be quietly taken out of the way. I'll bet he gimmicked up that fancy scanner-proof gun of yours, too."

Fiolla was fast on the recovery, he had to give her that. She had already accepted what she had seen and revised her ideas accordingly. "That doesn't make any of this my fault," she pointed out logically.

Han didn't answer, being busy staring into the barrels and emission apertures of a variety of lethal weapons, doing his best to look friendly and unthreatening. He showed empty hands.

A man in unmatched tunic and trousers stepped up, disruptor in hand. His uniform wasn't regulation but he wore a starburst insignia on an armband. Han already knew from inquiries that Ammuud was run by a loose and often competitive coalition of seven major clans under Authority subcontract. From the disparity of uniforms and attire it appeared that all seven clans supplied men to the port security force.

"What's the meaning of this?" the leader snapped. "Who are you? What happened up there?" On that last he gestured toward the sky over Ammuud with his pistol barrel.

Han dropped down from the open hatch and casually but conspicuously raised his hands while donning his sunniest smile. "We were passengers on the liner *Lady of Mindor*. She was attacked and boarded by pirates; we two escaped, but I don't know what happened after we left."

"According to screens, the pirate has cut loose from that liner and run; we haven't got a paint on it anymore. Let me see your identification, please." The man hadn't lowered his sidearm.

"We didn't have time to pack our bags," Han told him. "We jumped the first lifeboat we came to and got clear."

"And just in time," added Fiolla, poised at the hatch. "Please help me down, darling?"

Several of the port police automatically closed in to assist. Fiolla looked very good, even with her gown ripped and dust from the utility core on her. She also added a convincing note to Han's story. He interceded before anyone else could help and, hands at her waist, lowered her to the field.

The officer in charge began rubbing his forehead. "It looks as if I'll have to take you to the Reesbon stronghold for further questioning."

But one of his men objected. "Why to the Reesbons'? Why not to our clan stronghold, the Glayyds'? There are more of us here than you."

Han recalled that Reesbon and Glayyd were two of the six controlling clans here on Ammuud. And the Mor Glayyd, patriarch of his clan, was the man Han and Fiolla were here to see. A quick look around indicated to him that the *Falcon* didn't seem to be on the field. Han resisted the impulse to inquire about his ship, not wanting to implicate Chewbacca in what was going on if he could avoid it.

But the problem of the moment involved being carted off to some clan stronghold. He wasn't sure yet what he would say to the Glayyd leader, but he knew

he had no desire to be sequestered in the family home
of the Reesbons.

"Actually, I'm here because I have business to con-
duct with the Mor Glayyd," he commented. That
drew a scowl from the officer but, to Han's surprise,
also evoked a suspicious look from the Glayyd men
and women.

The first Glayyd clansman spoke again. "There, you
see? Do you deny that this is something that can be
investigated by the Mor Glayyd just as honestly as by
the Mor Reesbon?"

The officer and his kinsmen were in the great mi-
nority; he saw he could win neither by rank nor force.
Han had the impression the port police forces were
shot through with dissension. The officer's lips compressed as he conceded the point stiffly. "I will summon a ground car; we'll have to keep all the weapons
vehicles here at the port."

Just then a slow metallic voice behind Han drawled,
"Sir, hadn't I best come with you? Or would you
rather I remained here with the boat?"

Han did his best to keep his jaw from dropping.
Bollux stood in the lifeboat's hatch, to all intents
awaiting orders after an eventful descent and landing.

"I thought you two were alone?" said one of the
port police with a hint of accusation.

Fiolla was faster on the uptake than Han. "There's
just us and our personal 'droid," she explained. "Do
the Ammuud clans count machinery among the clan
populace?"

Han was still staring at Bollux; he couldn't have
been more surprised if the 'droid had danced his way
out of a party-pastry. Then he got his brain into gear.
"No, you might as well come with us," he told the
'droid.

Bollux obediently lowered himself from the hatch.
The officer was back, having spoken over the comlink
in one of the weapons carriers. "A car has been dis-

patched from the central pool and will be here very shortly," he told them. Turning to the Glayyd man who had given him the argument, he smiled bleakly. "I trust the Mor Glayyd will report on this matter to the other clans quickly. After all, he has other . . . pressing matters that may call him away soon."

The Glayyd people shifted and glowered, fingering their weapons as if the Reesbon officer had made an extreme provocation. The officer returned to his vehicle and, with the rest of the Reesbon people, departed.

The Glayyd man wanted to know more about Han's business with his clan leader. "No, he's not expecting me," Han answered honestly. "But it's a matter of extreme urgency, as important to him as to me."

To forestall more inquiries Fiolla leaned heavily on Han's arm, eyelids fluttering. Putting a hand to her brow, she did such a convincing imitation of being close to collapse that further questions went unasked.

"She's been through a lot," Han explained. "Maybe we could sit down while we're waiting for the car."

"Forgive me," muttered the Glayyd man. "Please make yourselves comfortable in the troop compartment of that carrier. I shall inform the Mor Glayyd of your arrival."

"Uh, tell him I'm sorry if we're taking him from something." Han was thinking of what the Reesbon officer had said. "What have we interrupted?"

The Glayyd man's eyes flicked over Han again. "The Mor Glayyd is to fight a death-duel," he said, and departed to send his message.

Seated with Bollux in the troop compartment, Fiolla and Han pressed the 'droid for information. He gave them a brief summary of events following their parting on Bonadan.

"What'd you do when the escape pod grounded?" Han wanted to know.

"I'm afraid Spray's timing wasn't all that good, sir," Bollux answered. "I landed some distance from the

city, but at least that kept me from being painted by
their sensor screens or destroyed on the way down;
defenses are very good here. I walked the rest of the
way to the spaceport and simply made myself inconspicuous, awaiting your appearance. I must admit I'd
been concentrating on incoming ships at their small
passenger terminal; I hadn't expected you to arrive
in this fashion. Also, I've managed to learn a good
deal about the current situation here."

"Wait; jet back," instructed Han. "What'd you
mean, made yourself inconspicuous? Where've you
been?"

"Why, doing what 'droids are supposed to do, Captain Solo," Bollux answered both of Han's questions
at once. "I simply entered the port through the labor-
automata checkpoint and began doing whatever work
there was to be done. Everyone always presumes that
a 'droid is owner-imprinted and task-programmed.
After all, why else would a 'droid be working? No one
ever questioned me, even the labor-gang bosses. And
since I wasn't really assigned to anyone, no one
ever noticed when I drifted from one job to another.
Being a labor 'droid is very good protective coloration,
Captain."

Fiolla was interested. "But that involved deceiving
humans. Didn't it go against your fundamental programming?"

Han could have sworn Bollux sounded modest.
"My actions involved a very high order of probability
of contributing to your and the captain's well-being or
even, if I may say so, of preventing your coming to
harm. That, it goes without saying, overcame any
counterprogramming forbidding deception of a human. And so, when I saw your boat land, I simply
carried a shipping crate across the field until I was
behind your craft and then entered it through the rear
hatch. As I said—"

"Nobody notices a 'droid," Han anticipated him.

"When we're out of here I'll take care of that, if you like; we'll repaint you in flashy colors, how's that? Now what about this duel?"

"From what I've been able to learn listening to humans and talking to the few *intelligent* automata at the port, sir, there's an extremely rigid code of honor in force among the clans. The Mor Glayyd, leader of the most powerful clan, has been mortally insulted by an outsider, an extremely proficient gunman. The other clans won't intervene because they'd be happy to see the Mor Glayyd die. And, according to the code, no Glayyd family member is permitted to intervene either. If the Mor Glayyd fails to fight or his challenger is killed or injured before the contest, he'll lose all face and much of his popular support, and violate his oath as clan protector."

"We've got to get to him before this stupid duel," Fiolla exclaimed to Han. "We can't afford to have him killed!"

"I'm sure he feels the same way," Han assured her dryly. Just then a car slid up, a wide, soft-tired ground vehicle gleaming a hard, enamel black.

"I've changed my mind," Han told the Glayyd clansman. "My 'droid here will stay with the lifeboat. After all, it's not my property and I guess I'll be responsible for its safe return."

There was no objection. Bollux re-entered the boat and Han and Fiolla made themselves comfortable in the car's deeply upholstered interior. Glayyd clanspeople caught handholds and mounted the car's running boards.

The car was warm and comfortable, with enough room for a dozen passengers. A driver, backed by a guidance computer, sat on the other side of a thick transparisteel partition. The ride took them through the main part of the city. It was a rather ramshackle affair, its buildings being more often of wood or stone than of fusion-formed material or shaped formex.

Street drainage was provided by open gutters that were frequently choked with refuse and pools of crimson-scummed water.

The people they passed showed a wide range of activity. There were trappers, starshipwrights, forestry service police, maintenance trouble-shooters, freight haulers, and street vendors. Among them jostled the young men of the clans and their carefully chaperoned kinswomen.

For all its faults and imperfections, Han preferred an open, brawling, and vital place like Ammuud to the depressing functionality of a Bonadan or the groomed sterility of one of the Authority's capitol worlds. This place might never be awash in profit or influential in galactic affairs, but it looked like an interesting place to live.

Fiolla frowned as they rolled past a row of slums. "It's an insult to have one of those eyesores in the Corporate Sector Authority."

"There're a lot worse things in the Authority," Han replied.

"Keep your lectures about what's wrong with the Authority," she shot back. "I'm better informed about that than you are. The difference between us is that I'm going to do something about it. And my first move is to get on the Board of Directors."

Han made a silencing motion, indicating the driver and the riders who clung to the car. Fiolla made a *hmmph!* at him, crossed her arms and stared angrily out her window.

The Glayyd stronghold looked like just that, a pile of huge blocks of fusion-formed material boasting detectors and weapons emplacements galore. The stronghold was set up against the rearing mountains at the edge of the city, and Han presumed that the peaks hid deep, all but impregnable shelters.

The car slid through an open gate at the foot of the stronghold and came to a stop in a cavernous garage guarded by young men, the Glayyd clan's footsoldiers. They didn't seem particularly wary and Han took it for granted that the car had been thoroughly checked out prior to admittance.

One of the clan guards escorted them to a small lift chute and stood aside as they entered, setting their destination for them. They rose quickly, and because the chute wasn't equipped with autocompensation gear, Han's ears popped.

When the doors swished open they found themselves looking out into a room far airier and more open than expected. Apparently some of those heavy blocks and slabs could be moved aside.

The room was furnished sparely but well. Robovassals and fine, if dated, conform-lounge furniture showed that the occupants enjoyed their luxuries. Waiting for the two was a woman some years younger than Fiolla.

She was dressed in a thickly embroidered gown trimmed in silvery thread and wore a shawl made of some wispy blue material. Her red-brown hair was held back by a single blue ribbon. She bore on her left cheek the discoloration of a recent injury; Han thought it the mark of a slap. She had a look of hope, and of misgiving.

"Won't you come in, please, and sit down? I'm afraid they neglected to forward your names to me."

They introduced themselves and found places in the comfortable furniture. Han wanted very much to hear her ask if he wanted something to drink, but she was so distracted that she ignored the subject altogether.

"I am Ido, sister to the Mor Glayyd," she said quickly. "Our patrolman didn't specify your business but I decided to see you, hoping it concerned this . . . current distress."

"Meaning the death duel?" Fiolla asked straight-forwardly.

The young woman nodded. "Not us," Han said

quickly, to keep the matter clear. Fiolla gave him a
caustic look.

"Then I don't think my brother will have time to
speak to you," Ido went on. "The duel has been twice
postponed, though we hadn't expected that, but no
further delay will be allowed."

Han was about to argue but Fiolla, more the dip-
lomat than he, changed the course of conversation for
the moment, asking what had prompted the challenge.
Ido's fingertips went to the mark on her face.

"This is the cause," she said. "I fear this little mark
is my brother's death sentence. An offworlder appeared here several days ago and contrived to be
introduced to me at a reception. We took a turn
through the roof garden at his invitation. He became
enraged at something I said, or so it seemed. He
struck me. My brother had no choice but to make
challenge. Since then we've learned that this fellow is
a famous gunman who has killed many opponents.
The whole thing seems a plot to kill my brother, but
it's too late to avoid the duel."

"What's his name, the offworlder?" Han asked, interested now.

"Gallandro, he is called," she replied. Han didn't
recognize the name but, oddly enough, he saw from
Fiolla's face that she had. *She keeps track of some
strange information,* he thought.

"I'd hoped you might have come to prevent the
duel or intervene," Ido said. "None of the other clans
will, since they envy us and would like to see us in
misfortune. And by the Code, no one else in our clan
or its service can take my brother's part. But another
outsider may, for the sake of either our interests or
his own. That is to say, if it's a matter that directly
concerns him."

Han was thinking that if he were the Mor Glayyd
he'd be shopping around for a fast starship with the
family jewelry in his pocket. His musings were inter-

rupted by Fiolla's voice. "Ido, please let us talk to your brother; there may be something we can do."

After Ido, overjoyed, had rushed away, Han, ignoring the possibility of listening devices, exploded. "What's wrong with you? What can *you* do to help him?"

She stared back blithely. "I? Why, nothing. But you can take his place and save him."

"Me?" he howled, coming to his feet so quickly that he nearly bowled over a robo-vassal. The mechanical skittered back with an electronic screech.

"I don't even know what the fight's about," Han continued at high volume. "I'm here looking for someone who owes me ten thousand. I never heard of either of these people. Which reminds me, it looked like you knew about the gunfighter, what's his name—"

"Gallandro, a name I've heard before. If it's the same man, he's the territorial manager's most trusted operative; I've only heard his name once before. Odumin, the territorial manager, must be involved in all this; these must be the 'measures' Magg informed Zlarb about. If Gallandro kills the Mor Glayyd, it'll end your tracing of Zlarb's bosses and your chance to collect. But if you intercede for the Mor Glayyd, we might still get what we want."

"What about minor details," Han asked sarcastically, "such as if Gallandro kills me, for example?"

"I thought you were the Han Solo who said he could get more in this life with a blaster than with an open expense account. So this is your department. Besides, Gallandro will almost certainly withdraw when he finds out he'll have no chance of killing the Mor Glayyd anyway. And who'd dare face the great Han Solo?"

"Nobody wants to and nobody's going to!"

"Solo, Solo; you've eliminated Zlarb, seen Magg with the slavers, and heard what I've learned. Do you think they'll ever stop coming after you? Your one chance is to save the Mor Glayyd and get that information from him so that I can prosecute everyone connected with the slavery ring. And let's not forget the ten thousand they owe you."

"Let's not ever. What about it?"

"If you can't get it out of them, maybe I can get you some sort of compensation. Reward to a citizen for a job well done, commendation from the Board of Directors, that sort of thing."

"I want ten thousand, not a credit less," Han stipulated. Fiolla was right about one thing: unchecked, the slavers would undoubtedly keep coming after him. "And no ceremonial dinners. I'll leave through the back door, thanks."

"Whatever. But none of that's likely if you let Gallandro kill the Mor Glayyd."

At that moment the door swished open, and Ido returned, her hand through her brother's elbow. Han was surprised to see how young the Mor Glayyd was; he'd assumed that Ido was a kid sister. But the Mor Glayyd was even younger. He wore a fine outfit stiff with braid and decorations of one kind and another, and a gunbelt that somehow didn't look right on him. He was slightly shorter than his sister, slim and rather pale. His hair, the same color as hers, was caught behind him in a tail.

Ido made introductions, but while she referred to her brother by his title, she called him by a more familiar name.

"Ewwen, Captain Solo wishes to intervene for you. Oh, please, please agree!"

The Mor Glayyd was unsure. "For what reason?"

Han massaged the bridge of his nose with thumb and forefinger. Fiolla offered no hints, confident that he could come up with some plausible reply.

"I have, uh, business with you, a deal you might be interested in. It'll take some explaining—"

At that moment the comlink signaled for attention. The Mor Glayyd excused himself and crossed to the instrument. He must have activated a muting device as well; none of the others heard any part of the conversation. When he turned back, his face had become emotionless.

"It seems we lack time for your explanation, Captain Solo," he said. "The outworlder Gallandro and his second have appeared at the gate and will await me in the armory."

Steeling himself with *Think of cash!,* Han said, "Why don't I meet him for you?" When he saw he was going to get an argument out of this proud boy, he rushed on. "Remember your sister and your duty to your clan. Forget the point of honor; this is real life."

"Ewwen, please do," Ido implored her brother. "I beg it as a boonfavor to me."

The Mor Glayyd looked from one to another, almost spoke, held himself. "I couldn't yield this obligation to any member of my clan," he finally said to Han. "But my death would leave my sister and my kinsmen at the mercy of the other clans. Very well, I shall put myself in your debt. Let us repair to the armory."

The private lift chute carried them down quickly. The armory was a series of cold, echoing, vaulted rooms crammed with racks of energy guns, projectile firearms, and muscle-powered weapons along with work benches and tools with which to service them. Their footsteps resounded on stone as they made their way to a shooting range.

At the far end of the range and along the walls holotargets hung in the air, waiting to unfreeze into attack-evasion sequences. But it wasn't holotargets that were scheduled to be shot. At the nearer end of the range waited five people.

Han was fairly sure he could identify them—worlds with such an archaic and formal dueling code de-

manded about the same roster. The woman with the
weary look on her face and the professional medipack
slung from one shoulder would be the surgeon. In a
gunfight at close quarters, Han doubted that her duties
would extend beyond pronouncing the loser dead. ´

The older man in Glayyd household livery would
be the Mor Glayyd's second; he had a lean, scarred
face and was probably an instructor in arms or some
such to his clan leader. Another man, in what Han
had come to recognize as Reesbon colors, would be
the other second. There was a white-haired elderly
man standing aside and trying to conceal his nervous-
ness; he could only be the match's judge.

The last member of the group was easiest of all to
identify. Though Han had never seen him before,
the sight of him set off internal alarms. He was slightly
taller than Han but seemed smaller and more compact. Holding himself easily and gracefully, he wore a
somber outfit of gray trousers and high-collared tunic
with a short gray jacket over it. A trailing, supple
white scarf, knotted at his throat, fell in graceful tails
at his shoulder and back.

The man's graying hair had been cropped quite
short, but he had long mustachios hanging at the corners of his mouth, their ends gathered and weighted
by tiny golden beads. He was just in the process of
removing his jacket. An intricately tooled black gunbelt
encircled his waist, holding a blaster high up on his
right hip. He didn't observe the common practice of
studding his belt with a marker to indicate each opponent he'd beaten; he didn't look as if he needed to.

But it was the man's eyes that had set off most of
Han's alarms, making him absolutely certain of the
man's profession. The eyes were a deep, clear blue,
unblinking, unwavering. They examined all the newcomers, remained for a moment on the Mor Glayyd
and came to rest on Han, making a chilly estimate of

him in a moment. The look the two exchanged left little to be said.

"As challenged party," the Mor Glayyd's second was saying, "Gallandro has chosen a face-off draw rather than the measured paceway. Your favorite weapons have been prepared, Mor Glayyd. All weapons have been examined by both seconds."

Still meeting Gallandro's eyes, Han took the final step. "I have a call on the Mor Glayyd's time. It's my right to intervene for him, I hear."

There was a murmur among the seconds and judge. The surgeon merely shook her head tiredly. Han went to where the mentioned weapons had been set out and began checking them over. He had passed on a variety of fancy shoulder and forearm rigs and was debating between two gunbelts that resembled his own when he realized Gallandro was standing next to him.

"Why?" asked the gunfighter with a clinical curiosity.

"He doesn't have to explain," objected Ido, who was ignored.

"My dispute's with the Mor Glayyd; I don't even know you," said Gallandro.

"But you know I'm faster than the kid," Han said pleasantly, holding up a short-barreled needlebeamer for examination. Then he met Gallandro's gaze, which was as placid as a pool's surface at dawn. All the important information was exchanged then, though neither man's expression altered and nothing more was said. Han had no doubt the duel would proceed.

Instead, Gallandro turned and intoned: "Mor Glayyd, I find myself compelled to apologize, and tender you my earnest plea for your forgiveness and that of your sister." He stated his case indifferently, disposing of an unpleasant duty, and made little pretext of sincerity. "I trust that you'll pardon me and that this entire unfortunate incident will be forgotten."

For a second it looked as if the Mor Glayyd would

refuse the apology; having escaped a sure death, the boy wouldn't mind seeing Gallandro shot. Han was about to accept for him, not much inclined now toward a fast-draw contest, since it could be avoided.

But Ido spoke first. "We both accept your apology with the proviso that you leave our home and our homeworld as soon as possible."

Gallandro looked from her to Han, who still held the needlebeamer. Gathering his jacket, the gunman inclined his head to Ido and prepared to go. But he paused to trade one last hard look with Han.

"Another time, perhaps," Gallandro offered with a brittle smile.

"Whenever you can work yourself up to it."

Gallandro nearly laughed. Suddenly, he had spun, dropped into a half-crouch, drawn his blaster, and put four bolts dead-center into each of four holotargets along the wall. He had straightened, his sidearm spinning twice around his finger and ending up in his holster, before most of the people in the room had grasped what he'd done.

"Another time, perhaps," Gallandro repeated quietly He sketched a shallow bow to the women, the surgeon included, gathered the Reesbon second in by eye, and strode away, his steps carrying back to them loudly.

"It worked," sighed Fiolla. "But you shouldn't have traded digs with him, Solo. He seemed sort of —dangerous."

Han gazed at the four holotargets registering perfect hits, then back at the departing Gallandro. He ignored Fiolla's vast understatement. Gallandro was far and away the most dangerous gunman Han had ever seen; faster, he was nearly certain, than Han himself.

X

THE *Millennium Falcon* had found sanctuary by a small lake in a shallow valley high in the mountains beyond Ammuud's spaceport. Coming down the ramp, Spray was pleased to discover the previous night's windstorm had deposited no snow.

He found Chewbacca assembling an interesting collection of tools and equipment, including a metal tripod with telescoping legs, spools of light cable, supports, clamps, ground spikes, and a small sky-scan sensor unit. The skip-tracer inquired about the purpose of it all. With a few gestures, and growling in his own tongue by force of habit, Chewbacca made clear to Spray what he was about to do. In order to give them added protection, the Wookiee was going to mount the sky-scan sensor on the ridge line above them, where it would give a much wider area of surveillance than the *Falcon*'s equipment, surrounded by this little valley, could.

"B-but when will you be back?" Spray asked apprehensively. The *Falcon*'s first mate stopped himself from snorting derisively; the Tynnan had borne up well since the emergency landing and pulled his own weight, assisting in repairs and preparing meals. It wasn't Spray's fault if he wasn't used to survival living and wilderness situations.

Chewbacca made a quick motion with the tripod, as if spreading it and digging it in, and slapped its mounting plate, as if setting the sensor unit in place. The meaning was obvious; he wouldn't be gone long at all.

"But what about them?" Spray wanted to know, meaning the herd of grazers moving up the slopes from a lower valley into theirs. The shambling beasts went at their usual slow, imperturbable pace, feeding on scrub, rock lichen, and such spring grasses as were exposed, their antlered heads rising and dipping as they carried on their endless ruminations.

Several herds had passed through the area, neither showing any interest in the *Millennium Falcon* nor any hostility toward Spray or Chewbacca. The Wookiee spread his hands to show that the grazers presented no problem. Some of his equipment he tucked into the floppy carryall held against his right hip by his ammo bandolier; the rest he tucked into the loops of a tool roll, slipping it over his shoulder by its packstraps, then took up his bowcaster. Checking his weapon's action and magazine, he set off.

"And watch out for those things," Spray called through cupped hands, pointing aloft. The Wookiee looked up. As often happened, there were some of the pterosaurs of Ammuud, huge, long-beaked reptilian soarers, circling in search of prey. But, though they were usually to be seen singly or in pairs, perhaps a dozen of them were now quartering the sky.

The Wookiee looked askance at the skip-tracer and shook his bowcaster, snarling significantly; it was the soarers who would be well advised to take care. He set out again, his big, shaggy feet carrying him over the rocky ground and occasional patches of snow. His burden bothered him not at all.

He made good time and was soon leaning into the ascent to a high point on the ridge line. Atop it was a wide, level area and beyond the ridge was another, broader valley ending in a narrow pass. When he topped the ridge, Chewbacca spread out his tools and sat himself on a flat rock to begin assembling the sensor unit's tripod.

Once the mounting plate was locked into place on the tripod, he looked down to check on the starship. He couldn't see Spray, but that was no surprise; the skip-tracer was on the opposite side of the ship from the main ramp. What made his features cloud was the closeness of the herd of grazers; their main flow plodded within twenty meters of the freighter, though they showed no inclination to investigate or molest her. Too, this herd seemed far larger than any of the others; its leaders were well on their way to the pass, yet its end wasn't in sight. More and more grazers were making their way up from the lower slopes. But the calves were staying well to the center of the herd's mainstream, with the bigger bulls tromping along in the lead and on the flanks, and the whole group appeared orderly and moving leisurely. Satisfied for the moment, Chewbacca returned to his work, running a check to ensure the unit was charged and functioning.

When a distant thunder reached his sharp ears, his head snapped up at once. The grazers, so quiescent and unthreatening a moment before, were now in stampede. So far, they were sweeping wide of the *Falcon*, but the herd began ranging out, the front of the stampede widening as Chewbacca watched, becoming a sea of shaggy backs and a forest of antlers. The soarers were making sweeping dives in along the leading edge of the stampede, emitting eerie wailing sounds.

The Wookiee wasted no time speculating on whether the flying things had started the stampede with air attacks to cut out weaker or slower grazers. Snatching up his equipment, he took in the surrounding terrain, searching for some shelter. More grazers were galloping up from the lower slopes and the stampede gained momentum every second. The animals were no longer lumbering, clumsy shufflers; in flight, they were six-legged powerhouses, the smallest adult among them weighing four times what the Wookiee

did, traveling at high speed with the formidable im-
petus of fright.

But the narrow pass was already choked with struggling grazers, and as Chewbacca watched, the excess
began to mill in a tossing of antlers and fill the lower
valley. He put down his equipment and prepared to
run, only to discover that he was already cut off. The
grazers were flowing around the high point he had
selected, avoiding its steep incline on their way to the
lower valley.

A quick glance told him that the beasts were still
avoiding the unfamiliar bulk of the *Millennium
Falcon,* but if the backup from the pass reached that
far, their reticence could change. The Wookiee hoped
that Spray would have the sense to use the disabled
starship's weaponry to keep the animals from damaging her further. By that time, of course, the grazers
would be all over the ridge; they would start forging
up the steeper slopes as soon as the pressure of the
bottled herd grew great enough.

He held his bowcaster and took stock of his situation as objectively as he could, observing the animals
below and the terrain around him. At length he decided that to try to work his way through the herd or
even run with them would be suicide; they were
aroused and in panic now and would be quick to attack any outsider among them. On the other hand—

He broke off in midthought as a shadow passed
over him and a wailing cry warned him. He hit the
ground rolling, clutching his weapon to him. Broad
wings hissed through the air over him and sharp claws
closed on nothing. The soarer swept onward, leaving a
carrion reek in the air, screaming its frustration. A
second, behind it, tried a swoop of its own.

The Wookiee came up onto one knee and threw his
bowcaster up to his shoulder, lacking time to focus
through the weapon's scope. There was the high twang
of the bow, a simultaneous detonation as the explosive

quarrel crumpled the soarer's wingtip. The flier veered, crippled.

Chewbacca fell backward, jacking the foregrip of his bowcaster to recock it and strip another round off its magazine. He got two more shots into the predatory flier as it half-fell, half-flew past him, putting yawning wounds in its rib cage.

The creature tumbled, dead on the wing. It came down among the stampeding grazers and in a moment was gone from view, trampled into a shapeless mass by hundreds of hooves. Another soarer had glided in, sheered off when it heard the explosive quarrels and come around for another pass.

Chewbacca realized now why the soarers had come together in such numbers for the migration of grazers. The stampede through the wild mountain country would inevitably produce casualties, leave behind the weak or injured and, too, strand refugees like himself, ripe pickings for the airborne pack. The soarers' primitive brains had recognized the chance for a feast.

The Wookiee brought up his bowcaster again and carefully sighted on the oncoming soarer. It stooped for him, claws open, long, narrow beak wide with its cry. He centered it precisely in his scope and fired directly into the gaping maw. The top of its boney skull disappeared and it nosed down at once, plowing into the ground. He had to jump back out of the way as the soarer's corpse, seeming to collapse in on itself, slid to a stop where he had stood.

With two of their number down, the soarers were more cautious about approaching the ridge. They tilted membranous wings and put distance between themselves and whatever mysterious thing had killed their companions, searching all the while for more approachable prey. Chewbacca stole a look back down at the valley.

The press of grazers at the pass was backing up toward him quickly. Even now a few of the beasts were pausing to mill around the lower part of the ridge. The Wookiee fired several rounds into the ground there, blowing showers of soil and rock into the air and sending off the terrified, bellowing grazers. But the swirl of the backlogged stampede moved more animals in toward the ridge again; they were too scared and too stupid to notice the cause of the explosions of a moment before. He would never hold them back, even if he had unlimited ammunition.

A tremendous racket, rising over the cannonading hooves, came from the *Millennium Falcon*. It was the ship's distress signals—hooters and klaxons combined with flashing lights, designed to attract the attention of searchers in case of crash or emergency landing. Apparently the grazers had begun to get too close to the ship, and Spray had resorted to this to save her. It was good thinking on the skip-tracer's part, but Chewbacca knew he could look for little else in the way of help. He doubted if even the starship's guns could clear a secure path through the massed herd.

A soarer's cry sounded and he spied the creature rising from the cliff across the valley, bearing what looked like a stunned or injured grazer calf. The Wookiee growled an imprecation at the flier and wished for a second that he, too, had wings. Then he shook his fist in the air and bellowed wildly, for a mad inspiration worthy of Han Solo had just struck him.

As he worked out details, he slung his bowcaster and began rummaging through the equipment he had brought. First, the tripod. He clamped all three legs under his arm and got a firm grip on its mounting plate. Cords of muscle swelled in his arms and hands, and he gritted his fierce teeth in exertion. Slowly, he put the needed crease into the tough metal of the plate.

When he was satisfied, he put down the tripod and began to work furiously, casting occasional glances down to the growing turmoil in the valley as it surged toward his high ground. He had, he believed, the tools and materials he required; time was another question entirely.

He threw the downed soarer's carcass over onto its back without trouble; its bones were hollow and it had, for all its size, evolved for minimum weight. He jammed the bent mounting plate up under its chin, ignoring the ruin of its gaping skull, and fixed it there with a retainer from his tool roll, turning its screw down as tightly as he could without crushing the bone.

He spread two of the tripod's legs, extending them to maximum length, and lay them out along each wing. He curled the leading edge of the wings over the tripod legs and wrapped them two full turns at the tips, exerting his strength against the resistance of the wing cartilage. There was barely any fold at all near the wing joints, but it would have to serve. He had only eight clamps in his carryall pouch; four for each wing had better be enough. He tightened them down quickly to hold the tripod legs in place within the folds of the wing edges.

Stopping to check, he saw that the grazers were already thronging on the lower slopes of his high ground, packed tightly together, antlers swaying and flashing. He applied himself to his task with redoubled energy.

He drew the central tripod leg out along the soarer's body as a longitudinal axis. The creature was an efficient glider, but its breast lacked the prominent keel to which flight muscles are attached in birds, and that made fastening a problem. He settled, after no more than a few seconds' thought, on a row of ring-fasteners punched through the skin and passed around the creature's slender sternum. Fortunately, it had no more than a vestigial tail. He swallowed and tried to ignore its nauseating odor as he worked.

Then came his worst problem, a kingpost. Taking one of the bracing members he had brought, he thrust it up directly through the soarer's body next to the sternum, to stand a meter and a half out its back, and made it fast to the longitudinal axis. Then he fit the longest brace he had across the juncture, securing it to the other two tripod legs as a lateral axis. He didn't fret over the various vile substances now leaking out of the soarer; that decreased the weight, which could only help.

He spent a frantic several minutes cutting and fitting cable, with no time to measure or experiment, connecting wingtips, tail, and beak to the tip of the kingpost.

He had to pause when a group of grazers breasted the ridge, wild-eyed and quick to swing their antlers in his direction. He jammed a new magazine into his bowcaster and emptied it into the ground, filling the air with explosions that could be heard over the countless hoof-falls in the valley, driving the animals back down for the time being. But the valley was now filled and there would be no room for them below, he knew; it was only a matter of moments before a major part of the stampede covered the high ground and engulfed the Wookiee.

The soarer's grasping legs probably hadn't given it very good locomotion, but they made a plausible control bar once Chewbacca had stiffened them with supports, wired the claws together, and braced the shoulders with ground spikes. Then they, too, were cabled to wingtips, nose, and vestigial tail. The Wookiee dashed around the soarer's body, tightening down turnbuckles with no more than a hasty guess at the tension needed.

He heaved, thews bulging under his pelt, and lifted the animal framework, gazing down and hoping the stampede had receded and that he would be spared the necessity of testing his handiwork.

It hadn't; grazers were literally being borne up toward him by the pressure of those below. Another barrage from the bowcaster only made them fall back for a moment; the tightly packed bodies came at him again.

Chewbacca took his ammo bandolier, twisted it several times to tighten it, then slipped both arms through it as a harness and fastened it together at the front with a length of cable, hooking himself up to the framework where kingpost met longitudinal axis. He shouldered the weight of the soarer and slung his bowcaster around his neck. The body slumped but the extremely light, superstrong support materials kept it in deployment.

A grazer bull with antlers like a hedge of bayonets cut in toward him. The Wookiee skipped out of the way and almost collided with another knot of the animals. The ridge was being overrun. With nothing to lose, Chewbacca churned toward a dropoff, holding the soarer's reinforced carcass at what he hoped was the correct angle of attack, and launched himself.

He wouldn't have been surprised if the wings had luffed and, with no lift at all, he had gone tumbling into the stamping, snorting mass of grazers. But a caprice of the strong air currents along the ridge flared the flier's wings, bearing him along on an updraft.

He began to yaw, the soarer's beak moving to the right, and pushed hard on the creature's braced claws to bring its nose around into the wind once more. Even so, his makeshift glider's sink rate was appalling. He raised his legs behind him and tried to distribute his weight for better control. He nosed up in an instinctive effort to get more lift, caring little about speed. He had flown powered craft of a design based on these same principles, but this was an entirely new experience. He nearly stalled and only barely got moving again.

Then a strong updraft off the ridge caught the soarer's wings, and a moment later he was truly flying. And for all the terror of unpowered flight, deadly

panic of the milling grazers below, reek of ichor dripping down cables and supports from the soarer's
corpse, the Wookiee found himself roaring and howling in elation. He started to dip the soarer's nose, but
the experiment with pitch nearly sent him into a neutral angle of attack—and an abrupt descent. He instantly foreswore the exploration of new aeronautical
principles.

Body centered, he made minor corrections and did
his best to recall the devotional chants of his distant
youth. Below him grazers thrashed and pushed, stri-
dent and frenzied, but the Wookiee now had the
sound of the wind in his ears. The other soarers
steered well clear of this new and bizarre rival. It was
large and strange and therefore not to be trusted.

Chewbacca estimated that he was making better
than thirty kilometers an hour and suddenly realized
he had but one problem—getting down alive. He had
angled toward the *Falcon*. The last of the herd had
passed it now, and the freighter seemed to be intact.
But his makeshift glider wasn't so inclined, and he
found that any decrease in speed threatened to rob
him of the lift that kept him aloft. Gradually, though,
he cut back on both, bringing the soarer's nose back
toward a neutral attitude, and brayed happily as he
spied a good landing spot. The little mountain lake
grew before him. He thought for a moment that he
was about to overshoot it and began to experiment
with a turn, hunching forward and pulling the soarer's
bound claws back toward himself.

He didn't quite have time to conclude what went
wrong; the next moment, Chewbacca and a splayed
carcass were gyrating toward the lake's surface. He
caught a split-second flash of his own reflection before
it parted for him with all the soft receptiveness of a
fusion-formed landing strip.

The curt slap of the water galvanized him, though,
helping him overcome the numbing cold. He fought to

HAN SOLO'S REVENGE   159

untwist himself, only to find that the soarer didn't float well; its wings settled around him and the weight of the metal framework bore him down. Reaching and wriggling, he still couldn't release himself from the improvised harness that held him to it. The bowcaster around his neck only complicated things.

He became snarled in slack cable and his giant strength meant nothing against the cushiony persistence of the lakewater. His breath, too much to retain, began to escape his lips in silvery bubbles as the Wookiee fought to free himself from the sinking glider. It became hard to see, and he found himself thinking about his family and his green, lush homeworld.

Then he realized a dark shape was circling him, making quick motions and weaving in and out among the tangled rigging with a sure ease and suppleness. A moment later the *Falcon*'s first mate was being tugged toward the surface of the lake, which came at him like an unending, flawed mirror.

Chewbacca broke into the air and drew a breath with such enthusiasm that he found himself choking on it, spitting and coughing and mouthing salty Wookiee expressions. Spray got around behind to support him, swimming with deftness and agility despite the pair of heavy cutters he held in one hand.

"That was fantastic!" gushed the skip-tracer. "I've never seen anything like that in my life! I came after you when I realized you'd overshoot and land in the lake, but I never thought I'd reach you in time. The land just isn't my element." He pulled at the Wookiee's shoulder to get him started.

Stroking for the nearby shore, Chewbacca decided he felt exactly the same way about the sky.

XI

"HIS name was Zlarb," Han said to the Mor Glayyd in that fortunate young man's study. "He tried to cheat me *and* kill me. He had a list of ships that were cleared through your clan's agency, but I haven't got the plaque with me right now. But if you could find his name in your records—"

"That isn't necessary. I know his name well," interrupted the Mor Glayyd, exchanging looks of extreme gravity with his sister.

"His bosses owe me ten thousand," said Han with something akin to fervor, "and I want it."

The Mor Glayyd leaned back, his conform lounger molding to him, and folded his hands. He no longer seemed quite so young; he was playing a role for which he'd been well groomed. Han wished he had hung on to one of those guns in the armory.

"What do you know of the clans of Ammuud and their Code, Captain Solo?"

"That the Code almost plotted your terminal orbit for you today," Han answered.

The youthful Mor Glayyd conceded, "A possibility. The Code is what holds the clans together yet keeps us from one another's throats. Without it, we'd revert to the backward, warring savages we were a hundred years ago. But betraying a trust or breaking an oath is also covered by the Code, and makes the violator a nonentity, an outcast, whatever his previous status. And not even a clan Mor is above the Code."

161

Oh, let me guess where this *is going,* Han simmered, but he said nothing.

"Those dealings my clan had with Zlarb's people fall into that category. We asked no questions; we accepted our commission for delivery and pickup of the ships without concerning ourselves with their use. Zlarb and his associates knew our practice; that's why they were willing to pay us so well."

"Meaning you're not going to tell me what I want to know," Han predicted.

"Meaning that I cannot. You're free to summon Gallandro back if you wish," returned the Mor Glayyd stiffly. His sister looked apprehensive.

Fiolla broke in: "Forget that; it's over with. But Zlarb's people broke faith with Han. Doesn't that mean anything to your Code? Do you shield traitors?"

The Mor Glayyd shook his head. "You don't see. No one broke faith with me or mine; that's the province of the Code."

"We're wasting our time," Han rasped to Fiolla. He was thinking of Chewbacca and the *Falcon.* He was willing to put aside his quest for the ten thousand for the time being; it didn't matter as much right now as the fact that Chewbacca was still somewhere out in the Ammuud mountains.

But as a parting shot he waved out at the city, at the departed Gallandro. "You saw what sort of people they are; you're throwing in with slavers and double-crossers and poisoners! They—"

The Mor Glayyd and his sister came out of their loungers so suddenly that the furniture slid on the slick floor. "How's that you say," the girl whispered, *"poisoners?"*

He'd said it thinking of the kit he had found on Zlarb and wondered now what nerve he had hit. "Zlarb was a Malkite poisoner."

"The late Mor Glayyd, our father, was killed with

poison only a half-month ago," Ido said. "Had you not heard of his death?"

When Han shook his head, the Mor Glayyd went on. "Only the most trusted of my clan circle know he was poisoned. It's unprecedented; the clans almost never use poisons, but we take precautions against them. And none of our food tasters showed any ill effects."

"They wouldn't, from Malkite stuff," Han told him. "Even some food-scanning equipment and air samplers miss it. And all a Malkite poisoner does to get around tasters is dose them with an antidote beforehand. The tasters never notice, and only the victim dies. Run tests on your tasters and I bet you'll find antidote traces in their systems."

He looked to Fiolla. "The poisoning must be the suggestion Magg spoke about in the tape I found on Zlarb; I don't know how the duel bears on it."

The Mor Glayyd had been rocked by what he'd heard. "Then, then—"

His sister finished for him. "We, too, have been betrayed, Ewwen."

Han Solo checked his pocket to make sure the plaque given him by the Mor Glayyd was secure and tugged at the too-tight collar of the suit he had borrowed. Bollux was just finishing loading the lifeboat with guidance components—shielded circuitry rather than those damned fluidics!—provided from his own repair shops by the Mor Glayyd.

The boat had been moved here to the Glayyd yards so that its departure would be less conspicuous. The Mor Glayyd had shown a grim openhandedness when quick tests had borne out Han's suspicion that the food tasters' bodies contained traces of a Malkite antidote.

"You're certain you don't want us to accompany you?" the boy was saying for the fourth time.

Han declined. "That would draw too much attention if the slavers or the other clans are watching. I just hope the port defenses don't burn us out of the sky."

"Many of my people are on watch today," the Mor Glayyd answered, "and you're listed as a regular patrol flight over hereditary Glayyd lands. You'll go unchallenged. We'll be listening; if you need us, we'll come as quickly as we can. I'm sorry that your *Millennium Falcon* dropped beneath the detection ceiling when she bypassed the spaceport."

"No stress; I'll find her. But they should be getting the *Lady of Mindor* repaired any time now. Right after that, this place'll be alive with Espos. Do you think you can stall them?"

The Mor Glayyd was mildly amused. "Captain Solo, I thought you understood; my people are *very* good at not answering questions. None will violate the Silence, especially to Security Police."

Fiolla joined them. Like Han, she wore a borrowed Glayyd flier's snugsuit of gleaming blue and high spacer's boots. She'd been both awed and angered when she'd seen the names of Authority higher-ups who were implicated in the slaving ring by the Glayyd records, though the evidence was a bit tenuous, mostly official permits for ship charters and certifications for operation within the Authority.

"Please remember, Fiolla, we expect to hear from you when you've rooted out our enemies," the Mor Glayyd said. "If we can't work our own vengeance we will at least witness yours."

She promised soberly, "You will—and I know what a vow means to the Mor Glayyd. When I've gotten all this before an Authority Court I think I'll be able to keep you from prosecution. But I'd advise you to scrutinize future clients more closely."

The Mor Glayyd raised his hand in farewell. "We will not be used again, you may be confident." Ido kissed both Han and Fiolla on the cheek. Then brother and sister stepped back, as did their kinsmen and kinswomen. Within seconds the lifeboat lifted from its resting place, drifted into a departure lane, and sped up toward the mountains above the spaceport, hurtling between them and rising for the higher peaks beyond.

"How are you going to find them, anyway?" Fiolla, again in the copilot's seat, asked. "The sensors and detectors in this kettle aren't made for a tight search, are they?" She moved aside a disruptor rifle given them by the Mor Glayyd, to give herself more room.

Han laughed, happy to be off the ground again. "This wreck? You'd be lucky to find your own back pocket with the gear she carries. Even if she had a whole scoutship package, there'd be all these peaks and valleys and the ground clutter. But we've got this," he put a forefinger to his temple dramatically.

"If we haven't got something a little more high-powered than *that*," she said, mimicking his gesture perfectly, "I hope there are some drop-harnesses aboard, because I want out!"

Han brought the little craft over onto a prechosen course, satisfied that he'd dipped low enough behind the peaks to be off the spaceport's detectors. "We know the course Chewie was on when he passed over the port and *I* know how he thinks, how he pilots. I am now Chewie, with a damaged *Falcon* under me, one I've got to keep above three thousand meters, with limited guidance response. I know his style well enough to duplicate it. For instance, he'd never bank right off those three high peaks up there. You can't see enough of what's beyond to be sure of finding a high enough landing place to set down without blowing the rest of the fluidics.

"The *Falcon* would have enough emergency thrust to take the other cliff, and the terrain layout says there'll be more open space over there; you can see more of what you'd be getting into. That's the way my cautious old Wookiee pal likes things. He'll be looking for an out-of-the-way spot where he can set down, keep out of sight, try to do some repairs himself, and wait for me. I'll find him, don't worry."

"You call this a plan?" she scoffed. "Why don't we just buzz along yelling his name out the hatch?"

His tone sharpened. "I said *I'd find him!*"

Then Fiolla understood what desperate fears for Chewbacca's safety Han had been suppressing. "I know you will, Han," she added quietly.

Spray, the skip-tracer, wound his sinuous body through the chilly water, fully at home, indulging in aquabatics and playful zigzags for the sheer joy of it, his tapered tail and webbed paws driving and guiding him with grace and power, his nostrils clenched shut tightly. The clear water in this small mountaintop lake, fed by underground springs and runoff, was cold even by Spray's standards, but his pelt kept him comfortable enough for short swims. As a youth, he had swum in much colder water, but he hadn't had the leisure for much swimming in a long time.

At last the Tynnan saw what he was looking for, one of the multilegged crustaceans that made its home in the lake's bottom. Spray was a bit short on air, having been frolicking when he should have been searching, he realized a little guiltily. He put on a burst of speed, hoping to catch the creature without a prolonged chase.

The crustacean didn't sense Spray's shadow or the pressure-wave he threw out before him until it was too late. It had barely begun to pick up speed when Spray seized it from behind—carefully, to avoid the pincers and walking legs. The velocity of his dive carried him down nearer the lake's bottom where, to his great surprise, his shadow scared up a second crustacean.

With a happy burble at the thought of the good

lunch he would provide, Spray struck and doubled his
catch for the day. When his air supply approached its
limit, Spray headed for the lake's surface. He broke
through with a happy squeal, spitting a jet of water
high into the air and filling his lungs again.

He held his catch over his head, treading water
and waving the crustaceans at Chewbacca, who stood
on the shore. The Wookiee woofed happily and hun-
grily and waved back. By the time Spray was wading
ashore, the *Falcon*'s first mate was already knee-
deep in the cold water, holding an empty toolbag wide open. Spray dropped his prizes into the bag
gingerly, and Chewbacca shut it at once; he ruffled
the skip-tracer's furry head in approval. "You came
along at just the right moment," said the Tynnan.

The freighter's rations had been all but depleted
when Chewbacca had set her down, and no grazers
had come near since the stampede. But Spray's skill
had kept them fed, and they had split their tasks—
Chewbacca staying busy with repairs and Spray taking on the job of meal procurement. Now they turned
back for the half-kilometer trudge to the grounded
starship. Water was already bubbling in an old inducer
cowling that Spray had set over a thermal coil at the
ramp's foot.

Their contemplation of a tasty meal was broken
when Spray's head perked up, his ears swinging this
way and that. Chewbacca craned at the sky and
pointed, woofing an exclamation. A small boat or
large gravsled had just crested the ridge and was now
dropping in directly toward them.

The Wookiee pressed the toolbag into Spray's
hands, leaving his own free to unsling his bowcaster.
Not that the weapons would be much good against an
aircraft, he reminded himself, as there was no cover
near them. Luckily, Spray had the sense to imitate
Chewbacca in remaining perfectly still. He realized

that movement, more than anything else, would attract the attention of the airborne observer.

The boat passed over them, but even as it did, Chewbacca could hear the strain of its steering thrusters as its pilot came about for another pass. He pivoted, watching, then barked and roared with pleasure. On its second pass the boat waggled and went into a barrel roll. It could only be Han Solo.

Chewbacca plunged through the snow toward the freighter, yowling at the top of his lungs, making the shallow valley echo. Spray, clutching the writhing toolbag to his chest, followed in the Wookiee's wake as best he could.

When the lifeboat had settled next to the *Falcon,* its lock opened and Han jumped out. Chewbacca raced to him, kicking up an aftermath of churned snow, and began pounding his friend on the back and howling his delight across the valley from time to time. When the first wave of joy had passed, the Wookiee noticed Fiolla at the boat's hatch. He plucked her down and whirled her around in a carefully restrained hug, then set her on her feet.

Last to descend was Bollux. To him Chewbacca extended a friendly growl but withheld a helping paw, not wanting to imply that the 'droid needed assistance. A rumble of inquiry from the Wookiee and a thumb indicating Bollux's chest panels brought assurances that Blue Max, too, was present.

"We almost passed you by," Han said. "You're a little too good at camouflage." He meant the *Millennium Falcon,* which Chewbacca had permitted to settle until her landing gear was nearly retracted. The Wookiee and Spray had piled snow around the starship and spread clumps of scrub and more snow across her upper hull.

"But we noticed all those animal tracks detouring around to either side of her," Han added, "so I took a closer look." Spray and Chewbacca were tug-

ging at the arrivals, urging them to come aboard. Han
delayed just long enough to drag forth some of the
new circuitry; he thought for a moment his copilot was
going to weep at the sight of it.

Lunch was forgotten as they brought one another
up on what had happened. Spray turned sheepish
when his jettisoning of Bollux was mentioned. "To tell
the truth, Captain," he said, "as I explained to Chewbacca here, I got the idea all at once and knew I'd
have to act instantly." To the 'droid he said, "I truly
apologize, but it seemed like the only thing to do, and
I sometimes have trouble making snap decisions. I
just plunged ahead with it before I could stop and
dither. Perhaps the general impulsiveness was con-
tagious."

"I fully understand, sir," Bollux answered gra-
ciously. "And as it worked out, it was quite fortunate
for all of us that you thought and acted so quickly.
Blue Max agrees with me, too."

They all thought it best to ignore the high-pitched,
hollow sounding *"Hah!"* that came from Bollux's
closed chest panels.

Soon they were all at work. Bollux, Spray, and
Fiolla began clearing away what they could of the
piled snow, concentrating on exposing the cockpit,
bow, and main thrusters. Han and Chewbacca strained
at repairs with Blue Max, out of Bollux's chest emplacement and connected to the forward tech station
to check for accuracy as each individual hookup was
made.

As the fluidic components were removed one by
one from the starship, Chewbacca took great pleasure
in heaving them as far as he could; some of his
throws were so impressive that Han regretted that it
wasn't a formal athletic event. He pardoned his friend
these excesses; the fluidics had been as much a curse
as a blessing since they were installed.

As the replacements were made, the pile of dis-

carded adaptors and jury-rigged gear grew. Because
they knew intimately every cubic centimeter of their
ship, they worked rapidly; they had originally installed
the fluidics in such fashion that removal would be
simple.

Activating another component, Han asked Max
over the comlink how things looked from the tech
station. "Checks out perfectly, Captain," came the
computer's childish voice.

Pleased with the speed with which their labors were
going, Han said, "We should take time to retune the
engine power-curves for peak efficiency, but I'd
rather get off Ammuud first. The biggest job's the only
one left—the hyperspace control units. Shouldn't take
more than—"

"Captain Solo!" Max's vocoder communicated urgency. "Trouble! Long-range sensors paint three
blips!"

Chewbacca yipped a question at Han, who
snapped a sharp response. "What's it matter who they
are? They're not coming for a gala sendoff, that's for
sure. No time for the hyperdrive. Seal up the hull."
He called to Fiolla and the others "Get aboard; we're
raising ship right now!"

Han sprinted up the ramp, leaving his first mate to
close up the exposed systems. In the cockpit his hands
flew back and forth across both his own and Chewbacca's sides of the console. Among other things, he
flicked on the ship's commo board and monitoring
outfit, though he doubted he'd pick up much in the
way of transmissions from the bogies.

But a moment later, in the midst of charging the
ship's weaponry, he noticed a blinking telltale on the
broad-band monitor. He read the instruments;
there was a steady signal coming from somewhere
very close by. A fast scan by the direction finder told
him its origin.

He recalled that he had left the disruptor rifle in

the lifeboat. But Chewbacca had placed his gunbelt in the navigator's chair. Good boy! Fastening the belt around his hips and tying down the holster, he rushed back for the ramp.

Chewbacca noticed the blaster at once. "We've been popped," Han explained. "Somebody keyed the boat transceiver; we've been sending all along. It probably took them this long to pick us up among all the dips and crags." He was glaring meaningfully at Fiolla.

"After all this time," she said with amazement, "you still don't trust me."

"Name another nominee? Spray hasn't been near the boat and I sure don't remember doing it." He beckoned his partner. "We've got work to do, pal. Spray, you too. Bollux, go with our other guest to the forward compartment and watch her. And brace your chassis for some rough weather." He started back for the cockpit, and Fiolla headed for the forward compartment without another word.

Han ushered Spray into the navigator's chair, directly behind his own, and all three buckled themselves in. He thought about sending out a distress signal to the Mor Glayyd, but a glance at the commo board ended that; one or more of the oncoming craft was jamming, and he had no time to try to circumvent the interference.

Bringing thrusters up to a hover, he retracted the ship's three-point landing gear the rest of the way. Over the low tumult of the engines he asked the Wookiee, "How good a pilot is he?" He jerked a thumb at Spray. The first mate made a so-so motion of his hairy paw but nodded, which meant that while the skip-tracer might never make the Kessel Run, he would be adequate in a jam—which this was. "Splendid," Han said unenthusiastically, and cut in main thrusters. Kicking up fountains of steam and mud and clumps of scrub growth, the *Millennium Fal-*

con blasted free of the remaining snow and shot off
into the sky.

Han let his copilot take the controls and left his
seat to bend over Spray. "Here it is: we haven't got
hyperdrive because we didn't have time to reconnect
it. That means we can't duck out of this one. Sensors
say those are small, fast jobs coming for us, maybe
interceptors, and sooner or later they'll overhaul us.
We can't outrun them but we can outfight them *if*
Chewie and I can man the turrets. That means somebody's got to pilot, so unless you feel like manning a
quad-mount—"

"Captain," gasped Spray, "I've never fired a
weapon in my life!"

"Sort of what I figured," sighed Han. "Take a seat
here." Scratching his hand nervously, Spray sat unwillingly in the pilot's seat while Han adjusted it and
pushed it closer to the console. Spray poked his bucktoothed snout up to various indicators, scopes, and
gauges; with his inferior eyesight he was, of course,
primarily an instrument pilot. But he obviously knew
what he was doing.

"Just keep shields up and try to angle with their
attack runs," Han instructed, "and try to preserve her
resale value, if that inspires you. Otherwise, nothing
fancy. Just leave the rest to us."

He and his partner made their way to the central
ladderwell that led to the top and belly turrets. "I wish
there was another way to do this," Han confessed.

"Dowwpp," the Wookiee responded.

Han climbed toward the top turret and felt the
vibrations along the ladder that told him his copilot
was descending. He hauled himself into the turret,
seating himself before the quad-guns and donning his
headset.

Ship's gravity was altered here, permitting him to
sit with his back perpendicular to the ladderwell without feeling a downward drag. In the same way, Chew-

bacca would be sitting in the belly turret facing directly "downward" without being pulled against his seat's belt.

Glancing over his shoulder, Han could look directly down the ladderwell at his friend's back. Chewbacca flipped him a quick wave, and each of them ran his battery through a few test-traverses, making sure the servos responded to control grips and tracked accurately.

"The usual stakes," Han called down, "and double for kills in the Money Lane." Chewbacca woofed consent.

Spray's voice, shaking with tension, came up. "I have three confirmed blips on approach. They should be on your screens by—*they're on us!*"

XII

JUST as Spray apprised the two partners of the on-coming craft, the newcomers announced their own arrival unmistakably. The *Millennium Falcon* quaked, her shields claiming huge amounts of power as cannon fire incandesced against her.

"They're breaking!" Spray yelled, but both Han and Chewbacca could already see that from their targeting monitors. Clutching the handgrips of his gunmount, Han traversed the quad-barrels astern to address his natural target, the uppermost of the vessels overtaking his ship. He knew the Wookiee would be on the one falling deepest into his own field of fire. They'd been through this sort of thing before; each knew the area of his responsibility and how the other worked.

The targeting computer drew up intersecting lines in two parallel grids and showed Han an arrowhead of light representing the bandit. From a lifetime's habit, Han divided his time and attention between computer modeling on the tiny screen and visual ranging. He never entirely trusted computers or any other machine; he liked to see what he was shooting at.

The target swept in, even faster than he had expected. It was, as he had thought it would be, a pinnace, a ship's fighting boat. *So, our friends the slavers are still with us.*

At the same time he was squeezing off quick bursts,

trying to bracket the pinnace. The quad-guns slammed away in alternating pairs, but the pinnace had picked up too much speed; it was into his gunsights and out again before Han had a chance to come close.

The starship shook like a child's toy as her defensive mantle struggled to deal with the blasts of the pinnace's cannon. Han registered, distantly, the sound of the belly guns and Chewbacca's frustrated howl as the Wookiee, too, missed on the first pass.

Then, instead of one triangle of light on his targeting monitor screen, Han saw two. He brought the quad-mount around hastily, its servos protesting, throwing him deeper against the padding of the gunner's seat.

A pinnace had come in from directly astern, its blaster fire bisecting the *Falcon*'s upper hull precisely. There were deep vibrations as the starship shuddered from the fire. Han couldn't stop himself, when he saw the volley walking along the hull at him, from throwing an arm up to protect himself. But deflectors held, and in a split second the pinnace had swept by with its two companions to come to bear for another run.

The pinnaces were perhaps twice the size of the lifeboat Han and Fiolla had stolen. They were fast, heavily armed, and nearly as maneuverable as fighters. Lacking hyperdrive, there was no question of outrunning them; the *Falcon* could only make a fight of it.

The freighter tilted and sideslipped as Spray attempted an evasive tactic. Han, his aim spoiled, yelled into his headset mike. "Nothing fancy, Spray. Just go with their strafing runs and cut into their speed advantage; no aerobatics!"

Spray trimmed the freighter. The pinnaces had broken right and left with the third ship going into a steep, rolling climb for an overhead attack. Han held fire, knowing they were out of range, and bided his time. Spray headed the freighter deeper into the high mountains.

The pinnace that had broken left now dove abruptly and came in under the *Falcon*'s belly. Han could hear the reports of Chewbacca's guns as he brought his own weapon around, its four barrels pivoting and elevating on their pintles in response to the commands of the targeting grips.

He tried for the diving pinnace. Outside the ball-turret the quad-guns responded minutely to the least adjustment of his controls. The computer limned aiming grids, plotted the pinnace's estimated course and speed, and predicted where it would be. Han slewed his seat around, hands clenching the grips, and four cannon barrels swung to follow suit. He opened fire and the quad-guns pounded red destruction at the bandit. He scored a partial hit, but the pinnace's shields held and it managed to evade his fire almost instantly.

"Swindler!" he howled, tracking the pinnace in a hopeless effort to connect again. There was the sound of a distant explosion and a triumphant roar echoed up the ladderwell. Chewbacca had drawn first blood.

The third pinnace swept past, taking a course almost at right angles to the one Han was still tracking. The newcomer got off a sustained burst that splashed harmlessly off shields, but there was a surge from the *Millennium Falcon*'s engines. The ship's defensive mantle was in danger of failing, having taken extreme punishment from the sustained, well-directed fire of the attackers.

Realizing he couldn't catch up with the one he had just missed and ignoring his comlink, Han yelled down the ladderwell, "Chewie! One in the Money Lane!"

Because of the *Falcon*'s design, a flattened sphere, and the position of her main batteries at the precise top and bottom of the ship, her turrets' fields of fire overlapped in a wedge expanding from the freighter's waist all the way round. This overlap was what Han and his first mate called the Money Lane; kills scored there counted extra, since it was a shared responsibility; their standing wager on who was better with a quad-mount carried a double payoff for hits in the Money Lane.

But right now Han didn't care if he ended up owing the Wookiee his shirt. Chewbacca brought his weapon around and just barely failed to get a bead on the pinnace out in the Money Lane, chopping the air behind it with crimson cannonfire.

"Spray, keep your eye on the long-range sensors," Han called into his mike. "If their parent ship sneaks up on us, Interstellar Collections will have nothing to auction off but a gas cloud!"

The ship missed by Chewbacca came up into Han's field of fire. He led it, reaching out for it with red cannon blasts, but the pinnace's pilot was quick and threw his ship out of the line of fire before his shields gave. The enemy scored on the *Millennium Falcon*'s upper hull, and the freighter bucked. Han caught the smell of smouldering circuitry.

"Captain Solo, there's a large vessel moving up rapidly from magnetic southwest. At current courses it'll close with us in another ninety seconds!"

Han was too busy to answer the skip-tracer. Hearing his first mate's frustrated growl at a near miss, reverberating in the ladderwell, he saw the ship the Wookiee had just lost. It arced out beyond the bow mandibles, its pilot going into a fast bank as he realized he'd flown into another line of fire.

Han didn't bother with the targeting computer but tracked by eye, catching the pinnace at the slow point in its turn with a sustained burst. A moment later the pinnace disappeared in a fireball, shreds of it hurled outward.

The third pinnace, coming about for another run, swerved to avoid the explosion of its companion, rolled, and was again in the Money Lane. Han's and Chewbacca's fire probed at it simultaneously. It, too, became an eruption of enormous violence.

Han was instantly at the ladderwell, not bothering to climb down but sliding with toes clamped to its side-pieces, braking himself with his hands, worrying about the oncoming mother ship.

As he reached main deck level, he found Chewbacca swarming up the rungs beneath him. The Wookiee crowed happily and Han found time to sneer "What d'you mean, *pay up? I* made the kill in the Money Lane; you never even touched him!"

Chewbacca snarled as they dashed together toward the cockpit, but the issue of who owed whom had to be dropped. Once Chewbacca was in place, Spray squirmed out of the pilot's seat, breathing with relief as Han dropped into it.

"That ship's coming at vector one-two-five-slash-one-six-zero," Spray said, but Han had already read that information off the console. Bringing the starship's helm over and accelerating, he angled all deflectors aft with one hand, belting himself in with the other.

Spray had taken on more altitude than Han would have liked. With the hyperdrive still inoperable, things boiled down to a simple race. His best chance to deny the enemy a clear shot at him was to put the planet between them.

He was still increasing speed, the engines' rumble growing louder and louder, when the *Falcon* was jolted by a teeth-rattling explosion. Checking combat information feeds, Han found that the approaching mother ship was firing from extreme range even though its shots had little chance of penetrating the freighter's shields at this distance.

Their pursuer was indeed the slaver, the would-be "pirate" that had stopped and grappled the *Lady of Mindor*. That left him nonplused about Fiolla's part in matters and why the lifeboat transceiver had been left keyed open. Surely the slavers were out to get Fiolla, too?

Then he had no more time for imponderables; the slaver ship was closing the gap between them and nothing he did seemed to make any difference. She was an extremely well-armed vessel, easily three times the *Millennium Falcon*'s size, and fast in the bargain.

If we had had time to retune the engines, Han carped at himself, *we'd be highstepping away from them right now.*

A voice crackled over the open commo board. "Heave to, *Millennium Falcon,* or we fire for effect!" Han recognized the voice.

He switched his headset to transmit mode. "No free meals today, Magg!"

Fiolla's onetime assistant said nothing more. The pursuer's shots came closer; the shields' drain on the *Falcon*'s power grew acute. Han trained batteries aft by servo-remote. The slaver with her heavier guns was still out of range. Though Han flew a twisting, evasive course, parting the cold air of Ammuud with a high whistle of speed, he knew the slaver would soon close. All he could hope for was that inspired piloting, more than a little luck, and a well-placed salvo to damage the slaver would get him clear.

He brought his ship out of a quick bank with a flourish, sideslipping as thick streams of turbolaser fire belched past to starboard, just missing the *Falcon*. He thought, *we could still make it, unless—*

Fulfilling his silent fear, the freighter wobbled and shook herself as if in the throes of a fit. Instruments confirmed that a brute tractor beam had fastened onto the *Falcon*. Her maximum effort failed to free her.

With the freighter held fast, the slaver closed rapidly. In another moment, Han knew, their pursuer would be on top of them. He tried not to be distracted by regrets; his hands flew across the console and he lacked even the time to tell his copilot what he was about to do.

Han brought the *Falcon* about at full power, just barely overcoming the drag of the tractor, redeploying defensive shields to maximum over the upper half of his ship's hull. Before the startled pilot of the slaver vessel knew what was happening, the *Millennium Falcon* had come about, reversing field in the tractor beam, and dived under his bow. Evading the tractor projector set in the bottom of the slaver's hull took an extra twist and full power from the freighter's already overworked engines, using both the tractor's draw and the *Falcon*'s thrust to snap-roll free of the beam.

Dumbfounded fire-control officers began redirecting their gun crews' aim, but the suddenness of the freighter's evasion had won Han the advantage of surprise.

Streaking under the length of the slaver, Han fired salvos from his top turret and waited with some dread for the moment his shields failed. But they didn't, and Han's wild aerobatics eluded all fire coming from the surprised slaver.

Nearly. There was a monumental jarring. Such of the *Falcon*'s alarms and warning lights as were not already alive came on. Chewbacca, taking damage readings, hooted worriedly as Han accelerated again, leaving the slaver to match him if she could.

He turned to Spray. "Some of that new stuff we put in today must've been hit; I don't get any readouts from it. Try the forward tech station and see if you can find out anything."

The skip-tracer staggered off, lurching this way and that as the ship swayed around him. Reaching the forward compartment, he found Fiolla and Bollux still seated in the acceleration couch. From the tech station's chair Spray began examining readouts

and squinting into scanners and scopes, twisting in the
chair and scratching at his hand nervously.

"Does your hand still hurt, Spray?" asked Fiolla.

"No, it's much—" he started to say, then stopped
and swung his chair around to face her with a shocked
look. "I meant—that is—"

"Somatigenerative treatments always leave the
skin itchy, don't they?" Fiolla went on, ignoring his
protests. "You've been scratching since we got here.
Solo told me he bit the hand of whoever jumped him
in the hangar at the Bonadan spaceport. It *was* you,
wasn't it?" There was little of inquiry in her tone,
more of statement.

Spray was very calm. "I forgot how bright you are,
Fiolla. Well, yes, as a matter of fact—" The *Falcon*
quaked again; the slaver was gaining on her once
more.

"And you left the lifeboat transceiver keyed open,
too, didn't you?" she snapped. "But how? Han was
right; you *weren't* anywhere near that boat."

"I did not," Spray declared soberly. "That, you
may believe. I hadn't expected things to go quite this
far, either; I abhor all this useless violence. This will
end soon; your ambitious former assistant is close."

Still not sure she credited any of what he had said,
she told him, "You know I'm going to tell Han, don't
you?"

Bollux turned red photoreceptors from one to the
other, wondering if he dared leave them alone long
enough to inform Han of what he'd heard.

Then the *Falcon* jolted again in response to a barrage. "I doubt if that would make any difference
now," Spray stated calmly. "And it's in your own best
interests, Fiolla, to cooperate with me; your life has
reached a critical juncture."

Han and Chewbacca had run out of options. The
slaver had fastened her tractor on them again. This

time there would be no survival value in a sudden reversal; the next volley would almost certainly penetrate shields and convert the *Millennium Falcon* into an explosive nimbus.

Han was busily training batteries for a last futile salvo in an attempt to avert death. But the volley didn't come. Chewbacca began pointing at the sensors and hooted excitedly. Han gaped, wanting to rub his eyes, at the size of the ship moving up hard astern the slaver.

She was an Espo destroyer of the old Victory class, close to a kilometer long, an armored space-going fortress. Where she'd come from wasn't as important to Han as what she would do.

The tractor beam pulling at the *Falcon* dissipated; the slaver had seen the destroyer, too, and wanted no part of her. But the Security Police battlewagon had tractors of her own, mightier than the slaver's. Suddenly the *Millennium Falcon* and her pursuer were both held in an inflexible, invisible grip.

Somebody aboard the slaver had the bad judgment to try a volley at the destroyer. Cannonade splashed harmlessly off the Espo's immense shields and a turbolaser turret in the warship's side answered, opening a huge hole in the slaver's hull and evaporating most of her power plant.

The slaver offered no further resistance. She was drawn up, uncontesting, into the gaping boarding lock in the destroyer's underbelly. The *Falcon*'s commo board sounded with a general override broadcast: "All personnel in both captive ships remain where you are. Follow all instructions and offer no opposition." There was something familiar about the voice. "Shut down your engines and lock all systems except commo."

Since the slaver was already occupying the destroyer's boarding lock, the *Falcon* was eased down toward the ground, the vast bulk of the battlewagon settling in over her, blocking out the sky. Relaxing to the inevitable, Han extended his ship's landing gear; the *Falcon* could never break from this tractor beam, and he had just seen the stupidity of trying to slug it out. He shut off his engines and cut power to weapons, shields, tractors, sensor suite.

He nudged his partner. "Keep your bowcaster ready; maybe we can make a break for it when we're outside." If they could get away, perhaps the Mor Glayyd could use a couple of good pilots. If not, there was nothing to worry about anyway, except which periodicals to subscribe to while in prison. But Han was determined to go out kicking.

The Espo craft descended until it was no more than fifty meters above the grounded *Falcon*. By leaning forward in the cockpit, Han could see the captive slaver ship. A boarding tube, no doubt packed with combat-armored Espo assault troops, was extending itself and fastening to the slaver's main lock.

Now, Magg, see how you *like it,* thought Han. It was only a knot of satisfaction in his long string of bad luck, but it was something. He savored it while he could.

From another lock in the destroyer a safety cage appeared, lowered by a utility tractor beam, coming down slowly and silently. The safety cage was a circular, basketlike affair with high guardrails and an overhead sling for hoist work. Within the cage, where Han would have expected a flock of trigger-happy Espos, there was only the man who had given the instructions over the commo a few moments before.

It was Gallandro, the gunman.

XIII

GALLANDRO approached the *Falcon* at a sedate pace. When he stopped, looking up at the cockpit, his hand moved to his belt and brought something up. A moment later the gunman's voice came over the commo board, obviously channeled through the Espo warship.

"Solo, can you hear me?" Rather than answer, Han flashed the ship's running lights once. "Oh, come now, Solo! How can you be surly to the man who saved your skin?"

Easily, Han reflected, *when he's so slick and so fast with a blaster.* But he opened his headset mike. "It's your play, Gallandro."

There was satisfaction in the other's tone. "That's better; isn't cordiality more pleasant? I'm sure that even you can grasp the realities here, Solo. If nothing else, you're a pragmatist. Kindly open your main hatch and come down, if you'd be so good, and we'll sort out this entire affair."

Han considered suggesting that Gallandro go sit in a converter, but one glance up at the great underbelly of the destroyer changed his mind. Turbolaser emplacements, twin and quad batteries, missile tubes, and tractor beam projectors were all aimed at the freighter. *One wrong move and we'll all be random energy.* He sighed and unbuckled his seat belt. Perhaps something outside would change the situation, but he knew nothing he could do there in the cockpit would help.

He turned to find that Spray had been standing at the rear of the cockpit, watching him. A moment later Fiolla appeared next to the Tynnan. It occurred to him that she might have some use as a hostage, but in view of the number of times her life had been in real danger already, he doubted that threatening her would deter Gallandro; the man seemed to know what real ruthlessness was. Besides, Han wasn't sure Gallandro would believe Han could kill her in cold blood, even now.

"Your friends have shown up," Han told her bitterly. "The Authority has things well in hand. There ought to be that big promo in this one, Fiolla."

She moved away toward the main hatch. Spray gave Han an odd look, then followed after. Encountering Bollux in the passageway, Han nodded at him. "Step into the cockpit and keep a photoreceptor on things, old-timer. If we don't come back the ship is yours, unless Interstellar Collections grabs it. Good luck; business has been lousy lately."

When Han got the hatch open he found Gallandro waiting at the ramp's foot. The gunman met his stare with a polite inclination of the head. "I mentioned earlier today, Captain, that there would perhaps be another occasion."

The invitation was obvious. Han thought about hooking for his blaster but, recalling Gallandro's incredible speed, set it aside as an option he could take later. Han was prepared to believe that the man confronting him was his equal or better with a sidearm.

Gallandro saw that in his expression and evinced a certain disappointment. "Very well then, Solo. You may keep your blaster for now, in case you change your mind. I don't suppose I need to tell you how many weapons are trained on you right now; please don't do anything abrupt without letting me clear it beforehand."

Han and Chewbacca stepped off to opposite sides of the ramp's foot, but Gallandro stayed far enough back to keep them both in view. The Wookiee, as aware of the situation as Han, kept his bowcaster slung at his shoulder.

Han was expecting to see a profuse greeting or at least a cordial welcome for Fiolla. But Gallandro accorded her only a suave smile and sketchy bow, and waited expectantly.

Spray was last down, coming at his slightly uneven dry-land gait, the tip of his tail brushing the ramp, some moisture from his recent swim still gleaming in his pelt. Gallandro bowed to him deferentially, although the gunman never lost sight of Han.

"Odumin," Gallandro said, "welcome, sir. You've brought yet another project to a successful conclusion. You haven't lost your touch for field work, I see."

Spray made a depreciating gesture, squinting up at the tall, aristocratic gunfighter. "I was fortunate, old friend. I must confess, I find I much prefer administration."

Han, who'd been gaping from one to the other while Chewbacca made little strangling sounds, finally got out *"Odumin?* You're the territorial manager? Why you treacherous, mutinous worm, I ought to—" Words failed him for a fate sufficiently horrible.

"That's hardly called for, Captain," Spray chided, sounding wounded. "I *did* start out as a skip-tracer, you see. But as I advanced myself in the structure of the Corporate Sector Authority, I found it expedient, as a nonhuman, to use others as go-betweens and remain an anonymous figure. In this slavery business, which extends to my own deputies and officials of the Security Police, I found myself obliged to do my own investigating with the help of a few trusted aides like Gallandro here."

He laced his webbed fingers together and assumed the introspective air of a teacher. Han found himself listening despite his fury.

"It was a very convoluted problem," Spray/Odumin

began. "First, there was the evidence that you had
taken off of Zlarb, which, you see, led you to Bonadan and convinced me that you were the slaver. At the
spaceport, when you headed for the hangar, I concluded that you were about to depart the planet. There
were materials at hand, a pair of work gloves and an
industrial solvent that could double as an anesthetic;
that prompted an overly hasty decision on my part to
attempt to take from you whatever information you
possessed in such a manner as to make you suspicious
of your, um, confederates. But you turned out to be a
resourceful man, Captain."

Han snorted. "I still can't believe you worked up
the guts to jump me, even with the lights out."

Spray drew himself up to his full height. "Don't
make the mistake so many others have; I'm more capable than I appear. With your superior eyesight neu-
tralized, you would almost certainly have grown dizzy
from the fumes before I; I can, after all, hold my
breath for protracted periods. But immediately after
our struggle, Gallandro here, who'd been running a
check on you, informed me of your true identity. I decided I'd found my solution."

Han's brows knit. "Solution?"

Spray turned to Chewbacca. "Remember our board
game, and the Eight Ilthmar Gambit, a lone combatant sent in to draw out an opponent? Captain Solo,
you were that playing piece, my solution. The slavers
knew you were no security operative and that you
couldn't appeal to the legal authorities. You compelled
them to acts that made them vulnerable, as you can
see, to me."

That made Han remember something else. He looked
to Fiolla. "What about you?"

Spray answered for her. "Oh, she's precisely what
she said she is: an ambitious, aggressive, loyal employee. The housecleaning required by this whole
business will leave some prime job slots in my organi-

zation; I plan to see Fiolla amply rewarded. My deputy territorial manager's position will be vacant quite soon, I should think."

"A plush job with the Authority," Han spat, "worst gang of plunderers who ever infested space."

"Not everyone can outfly them or rob them blind, Han," Fiolla said. "But somebody inside might bring change, as Spray's been trying to do. If someone had the right position, she might do a great deal of good."

"You see?" Spray's question was filled with approval. "Our attitudes are complementary. For all your daring and ability, Captain, you'll never do appreciable damage to an organization of the Authority's size and wealth. I submit to you that beings like Fiolla and myself, working within it, may accomplish what blasters cannot. How can you fault her for that?"

To avoid answering, Han looked to Gallandro. "What was the challenge all about?"

The gunman's hand moved in an airy dismissal. "The Glayyd clan constituted a particular problem; their records are connected to a destruct switch manned by loyal clan members. We couldn't risk going in and taking the evidence only to have it destroyed in the process.

"The elder Mor Glayyd mistrusted the slavers and they suspected him of planning to extort more money from them. They aren't the type for faith in human nature, you see. The slavers made secret overtures to the Reesbon clan and when the elder Mor Glayyd learned of it, he began making roundabout contact with Spray, fearing his clan was going to be betrayed. He was poisoned very soon thereafter, of course, partly at Zlarb's suggestion, as it seems.

"I preceded you all here; after the *Falcon* made her emergency landing, Odumin—sorry, sir, *Spray*—managed to contact me. I saw an opportunity to use the peculiar structure of their Code to put the Glayyds in your debt, Solo. It wasn't very difficult to make my-

self available to the Reesbons, and as far as they're
concerned, they're the ones who originated the idea of
having me challenge the new Mor Glayyd to a duel."

"A marvelous inspiration," applauded Spray. "And it
was also at your suggestion that the Reesbons contrived to key open the lifeboat transceiver?"

Gallandro shrugged modestly, twisting his mustache.
Han wanted to kick himself. And everyone else present. "Wait a minute, Spray," he objected. "How'd you
contact him? You were stuck out in the mountains."

Spray was suddenly chagrined. "Er, yes. There
were commo techs standing by for my signal, but I had
to have uninterrupted use of the *Falcon*'s facilities in
case Gallandro wasn't immediately available."

He turned to the Wookiee. "And that involves an
apology I owe you. To keep you away from the ship
for the requisite time I frightened those grazers into
stampeding with a flare gun, meaning only to isolate
you on the ridge for a time. I had no idea there'd be
so many of them, or that you'd be endangered. I'm
truly sorry."

Chewbacca pretended not to hear him, and Spray
didn't press the issue.

"So you're just another hired gun," Han said to
Gallandro. "Is that right? An errand boy on the Authority's chain?"

The gunman was amused. "You've got a lot of time
to put in before you're ready to pass judgment on me,
Solo, whereas I've been in your place already. I've
done it all, but I got tired of waiting to die in some
senseless manner. So I've given up sleeping with one
eye open, and in return I've got a future. Don't be
surprised if you feel this way yourself, somewhere
down the line."

Never, Han thought, but he found Gallandro to be
more of a puzzle than ever.

"With Magg and the others in the slaver ship, and
the evidence that's come to light, I should think our

case will be incontestable," Spray said with satisfaction.

"Then you won't be needing us?" Han said hopefully.

"Not quite true," the territorial manager admitted. "I'm afraid I can't simply let you go, though I'll do what I can to elicit leniency for you."

Han made a skeptical face. "From an Authority Court?"

Spray looked pained, squinting at Han, then away. Seeing the empty safety cage, he said, "Gallandro, did you bring no men? Who's going to fly the *Millennium Falcon* back to port?"

"They will," Gallandro announced, indicating Han and Chewbacca. "I'll go with them, to make sure they behave."

Spray was shaking his head vigorously. "This is sheer recklessness. Needless risk-taking! I know you didn't enjoy reneging on your challenge, but that was in line with your employment. There's no need to be provocative!"

"I will bring them," Gallandro repeated coolly. "Don't forget that I work for you under certain agreed-upon conditions."

"Yes," Spray lisped softly to himself, stroking his whiskers. He turned to Han. "This is Gallandro's affair; I cannot interfere. I advise you most emphatically against any rash acts, Captain Solo." He extended his paw, offering a friendship-grip. "Good luck to you."

Han ignored the extended hand, staring directly at Fiolla, who wouldn't meet his gaze. Spray looked to Chewbacca, but the Wookiee conspicuously clamped both hands on the sling of his bowcaster and gazed off into empty air.

The territorial manager sadly withdrew his hand. "Should you both succeed in avoiding imprisonment, I would advise you to leave the Authority as quickly as you can and never, never return. Fiolla, we'd better be

going. Oh, and Gallandro, please make sure you obtain
Zlarb's data plaque from Captain Solo."

He started off at a slow amble, tail dragging the
rocky ground. Fiolla fell in at his side without a backward glance. Gallandro extended his hand to Chewbacca. "I'm afraid I can't have both of you armed,
my tall friend. I'll take the bowcaster."

Chewbacca growled, showing long fangs, and might
have tried for a shootout right then and there. But
there was no doubt that the gunman could kill the
Wookiee where he stood and maybe get Han as well.
At least, Gallandro seemed confident he could.

"Pass it to him, Chewie," Han ordered. The
Wookiee looked at him, snarled again at Gallandro,
and reluctantly handed his weapon over stock-first.
Gallandro was careful to stay out of reach of those
shaggy arms. With a gesture to the ramp, he invited
them aboard.

"It's nearly that time, Captain Solo," said the gunman.

Just about, Han agreed to himself, and preceded
Gallandro up the ramp.

"Now," said Gallandro contentedly when they were
aboard, "if your copilot will be good enough to prepare the ship, you and I will get that data plaque." He
caught Chewbacca's eye. "Warm up your engines only,
and don't do anything rash, my friend; your partner's
life hinges on it."

The Wookiee turned to go and Han led the way toward his quarters. The cramped cubicle was in the
same disarray as when he had last seen it, with clothes
and equipment strewn on the sleeping pallet and the
tiny desk and chair. The pallet's free-fall netting had
somehow come unstrapped from its retainers and
hung from the bulkhead. A used mealpack tray sat
atop the desk reader.

Han ignored the clutter and stepped to his miniscule
closet as Gallandro put the bowcaster aside. With the

gunman watching him carefully, Han reached his right hand into the inner pocket of his thermosuit, feeling for Zlarb's security case. But as he groped for it he found that the case's clip was engaged, hooked through the top edge of the pocket.

That Wookiee's a big, ugly genius! Han thought, instantly covering the disarm button with his forefinger and drawing the case out, separating it from its clip. He offered it to the gunman.

Gallandro put out his own right hand willingly. It had occurred to him that Han might take advantage of the brief distraction and go for his blaster while Gallandro's right hand was on the case. He was more than happy to let Han try it if he wanted to. But while both men's right hands were still on the security case, Han simply moved his finger off the safety.

The two cried out as a surge of neuro-paralysis washed up their arms like an absolute-zero lightning bolt. The security case clattered to the deck as they both clutched numb, useless arms to their sides.

Gallandro gritted his teeth and glared at Han, who slowly and cautiously flicked open the tie-down of his holster. Gallandro's own left hand started for his holstered weapon but he realized what an awkward move it was and that Han hadn't gone for his blaster yet.

Han tugged at his gunbelt until his blaster sat, butt-forward, on his left hip. Gallandro, smile gone, did the same with his own tooled holster. Their hands were close to their weapons now.

"Had to change the odds a bit," Han grinned amiably. "Hope you don't mind. Whenever you're ready, Gallandro. The stage is yours."

The gunfighter's upper lip now held beads of sweat among the strands of his mustache. His hand began to tense, fingers preparing for the unfamiliar task. Han almost went for his gun then, but curbed himself sharply. Gallandro would have to be the one to decide.

The gunman's left hand drooped loosely, as he abandoned the effort. Chewbacca, unable to ignore the outcries he'd heard, appeared at the hatch. Han snatched the blaster from Gallandro's tooled holster and pressed it into his first mate's midsection as he dodged past him. "Hold onto him! I'm getting us out of here if I can!"

He was reading instrumentation from the moment he entered the cockpit at a full run. He stopped himself with the heel of his left hand against the console and vaulted into his seat. The engines were hot but, as per Gallandro's orders, guns, shields, and everything else but commo were cold.

The neuro-charge hadn't been crippling; the feeling in his right arm was already coming back. *For all the good it'll do me,* he frowned to himself. He was shocked at how little time had passed since he'd entered the ship; Spray and Fiolla had only now finished the long walk back to the cage.

He smashed his fist against the console. "Look at this! If I had firepower I'd have two perfect hostages under the guns. Or if I had tractors, I could haul 'em back here."

"There're other ways to handle cargo besides tractors," said a high-pitched vocoder. "Isn't that right, Bollux?"

"Blue Max is quite correct, sir," drawled the labor 'droid from the navigator's seat, from which he'd been keeping a photoreceptor on things, his plastron open. "As a general labor 'droid, I might point out—"

Han cut him off with a bloodcurdling war whoop and screamed back over his shoulder, hoping his copilot would hear, "Chewie! Hold onto your pelt; we're taking the long shot!"

He brought up full engine power. Giving the *Millennium Falcon* entirely too much acceleration, he tore off from a dead standstill to scream along under the belly of the destroyer, retracting landing gear as he went. Even with full braking thrusters he barely made a tight bank, throwing himself against the console as Bollux floundered for a handhold. Lining up his shot, he applied more power.

The safety cage, suspended halfway up to the access lock on its utility tractor, was before him with unbelievable speed. With more instinct than skill, Han made microscopic, split-second corrections in his course and hit braking thrusters again. The starboard bow mandible slipped through the cage's sling-arm.

Han accelerated again, carefully but extremely quickly, tearing the cage out of the utility tractor's grasp. "Go ahead, go ahead," he taunted the mountainous destroyer, whose weapons still tracked him. "Shoot me; you'll blow your territorial manager to *particles!*"

But no fire came. The *Falcon* shrieked out from under the Espo warship's belly; everything had happened with such suddenness that Han had snagged the cage before fire-control officers could decide what to do. Now they were powerless to intervene without endangering their superior. But the destroyer rose majestically and fell in behind the freighter in close pursuit.

Han was beside himself, laughing, howling, stomping his boots on the deck, but still piloting with utmost care; if anything happened to Spray and Fiolla now, the warship would surely eradicate the *Falcon*. He was relieved to find that the cage's sling-arm appeared to be firmly seated across the bow mandible.

Chewbacca appeared, pushing a ruffled Gallandro along before him. The Wookiee thrust the gunman into the commo officer's seat, then took his own. Gallandro was smoothing his mustache and straightening his clothes. "Solo, was it necessary to have this behemoth body-press me to the safety cushioning?" Then he noticed what had happened. Grudging admiration crept into his voice. "You seem to have gained the advantage, Solo. Congratulations, but please control yourself; the territorial manager is an extremely reasonable fellow and I'm sure he'll agree to any sane terms. I don't suppose that your unconditional release would be too much to ask. Oh, and perhaps afterward we can try that draw, for curiosity's sake. You may drain my pistol's charge first if you like; I'd just like to know what would've happened."

Han spared him a quick, disdainful look from the touchy business of guiding the *Falcon* smoothly and levelly through the hard, rocky peaks of Ammuud. "You *pay* to see the cards Gallandro; you folded."

The gunfighter nodded politely. "Of course; what could I have been thinking of? There will be other occasions, Captain. These circumstances were unique."

They both knew that was true; Han swallowed his next taunt. "If your arm's coming around, you can warm up the commo board and contact the commander of that gunboat back there. Tell him I want time and room to finish repairs on the *Falcon* and a little more on the side for a head start. No stunts now, or they'll be picking Spray up with blotters."

"Arrangements will be satisfactory," Gallandro assured him calmly, "with adequate safeguards for both sides." He set to work at the commo board.

Han cut his speed back, satisfied that there would be no fire from the Espos. He knuckled his copilot's arm. "That was a cute move. What made you rig up the security case's clip?"

The Wookiee answered with a string of the honks and grunts of his own language. Han turned his face back front, so his expression wouldn't show. It was highly unlikely that Gallandro understood any Wookiee, and he wouldn't know, unless he saw the pilot's face, how Chewbacca's reply had bewildered him.

Because Chewbacca hadn't connected the security

case's clip. And that left only one other person who had known where the case was. Han half-stood, half-leaned forward to look down through the canopy at the gently swaying safety cage. Spray was huddled miserably in the lowest corner of the dangling cage, webbed fingers clutched at the guardrail and its mesh-work. He was making a courageous effort, it seemed, not to become airsick as he pondered the sudden reversals of fate. Han figured that even with this turn-about, it had been a good day for the territorial man-ager; he resolved to trade grips with Spray before they again parted company.

Fiolla, unlike her superior, was braced more or less upright, clinging to the sling-arm and staring up at the cockpit. When she saw Han gazing down, a slow and secret smile crossed her face.

Knowing how well she could read the slightest kinetic movement, he mouthed *You are one very, very sharp future Senior Board Member.* He saw a laugh escape her then and she made a small, mocking bow of the head.

He pulled back down into his seat. Gallandro had raised the destroyer and was remonstrating with her skipper.

"I might just have to hang onto one of my hostages a little longer," Han interrupted. "To make sure you keep your end of the deal." Gallandro swiveled his chair around in surprise. "And don't get yourself in a lather, Gallandro; you'll get her back if your word's good." He went back to flying, checking sensors for a suitable landing spot. One more thought occurred to him.

"By the way, Gallandro, find out how much cash the purser has in his vault." He snickered at Chew-bacca's questioning bark. "What d'you mean, 'what for?' *Somebody* owes you and me ten thousand for services rendered. Or did you forget?"

Gallandro, teeth clenched, went back to his argument with the Espo captain. Chewbacca's happy guffaws rang as the Wookiee pounded his armrest, the vibrations traveling through the deck. Han leaned forward again and blew Fiolla a heartfelt kiss.

ABOUT THE AUTHOR

BRIAN DALEY was born in rural New Jersey in 1947 and still lives there. After a four-year enlistment in the Army and holding down the usual odd jobs (waiter, bartender, loading-dock worker), Mr. Daley enrolled in college, where he began his first novel. *The Doomfarers of Coramonde* was published in 1977; its sequel, *The Starfollowers of Coramonde*, in 1979.